Book donated by the GFWC
Woman's Club of the
Denville-Rockaway are

P9-BJB-773

Sister

Books by Ellen Howard

CIRCLE OF GIVING

WHEN DAYLIGHT COMES

GILLYFLOWER

EDITH HERSELF

HER OWN SONG

SISTER

Sister

Ellen Howard

A JEAN KARL BOOK

Atheneum   *1990*   *New York*

Collier Macmillan Canada
Toronto
Maxwell Macmillan International Publishing Group
New York   *Oxford*   *Singapore*   *Sydney*

Copyright © 1990 by Ellen Howard

All rights reserved. No part of this book may be reproduced or transmitted in any form or by any means, electronic or mechanical, including photocopying, recording, or by any information storage and retrieval system, without permission in writing from the publisher.

Atheneum
Macmillan Publishing Company
866 Third Avenue, New York, NY 10022

Collier Macmillan Canada, Inc.
1200 Eglinton Avenue East
Suite 200
Don Mills, Ontario M3C 3N1

First Edition
Printed in the United States of America
Designed by Nancy B. Williams
10 9 8 7 6 5 4 3 2 1

Library of Congress Cataloging-in-Publication Data

Howard, Ellen.
Sister/Ellen Howard.—1st ed.
p.   cm.
"A Jean Karl book."
Summary: Alena, the eldest child of a large family, remains hopeful despite the hardships of growing up on a farm in the late 1800s.
[1. Farm life—Fiction. 2. Family life—Fiction.] I. Title.
PZ7.H83274Si 1990   [Fic]—dc20   90-196   CIP   AC
ISBN 0-689-31653-4

For Cynthia Louise, Laurie Lee, Anna Elizabeth, and
Shaley Franc, sisters

and for Kristin Louise and Stephanie Lynn, sisters

and for my sister, Kathryn Alice

The author is grateful to the late Robert M. Cochran and to Barbara Cochran of the Hancock County Historical Society, Carthage, Illinois, for their generous help. Thanks are also due to Ruth Gash Taylor for her memories and suggestions.

Contents

Sister

❧ 1 ❧

First Day of School

ALENA WOKE EARLY to a breeze that ruffled the limp white curtains at the window. She felt it whisper, like a secret, across her bare legs. The night had been so hot there had been no need of covers. Now Alena luxuriated in the coolness of the breeze, stretching her legs out of her bunched-up nightdress, flinging her arms above her head. The coolness and the fresh smell made her think lazily of autumn and . . . Suddenly her eyes flew open. She sat up with a bound and swung her legs over the edge of the bed.

"Don't, Sister!" five-year-old Faith grumbled from the other side of the bed. Faith was curled in a plump, rosy tangle of round limbs and wrinkled nightdress. Her small face was screwed into a shut-eyed frown.

Alena laughed. She bounced on the edge of the bed, jouncing her little sister awake.

"Rise and shine, sleepyhead!" she cried. "Don't you remember what day this is? First day of school, that's

what! And Father says you get to go, too . . . if you get
out of bed, that is!"

Although Faith was little, and young for school, Father had indeed said she might start this year. "The
fewer little ones you have at home all day, the better,"
Alena had overheard him telling Mother.

Mother had said, "I'm only a little tired is all."

"Faith'll do fine at school," Father had interrupted.
"She knows how many beans make five. It's Alena
should stay home this year to help you. She's too old for
school anyways."

Alena remembered how her heart had frozen to hear
him say that. She had held her breath and waited, will-
ing her mother to speak. It had seemed to take a long
time.

Then, "It's her last year, Clay," Mother had said.
"It'd mean a deal to her to get a diploma."

"And it'd mean a deal to *you* to have help this
winter."

"I can manage. Alena comes straight home after
classes, and if Faith's in school, there'll only be the
littlest boys most the day." She laughed softly. "I
reckon I can handle two ragtag boys."

She can! She can! Alena was saying to herself. Of
course Mother could take care of the two youngest.
Mother had always taken care of all six children.

But what Father said next made Alena realize they
would soon be seven.

"I reckon you'd handle whatever you had to, Mary," Father said, his voice gruff, "but with another baby comin' and a girl 'most thirteen who could help, you oughtn't to have to. What good'll it do Alena, you suppose, that diploma?"

But I want it! Alena was crying silently. I *want* to graduate.

So when Mother said—"It'll do her *heart* good, Clay, and *mine*, too, for giving her one last year. She'll be doing for others all her life. Let her have this for herself!"—Alena felt a surge of joy and guilt, both at the same time.

Father *would* let her finish the grades. She knew he couldn't say no when Mother pleaded like that. Still, if Mother really *needed* her . . .

Then Alena had realized she was eavesdropping, and the guilt had multiplied.

But I *love* school, she had thought then and was thinking now as Faith scrambled up on hands and knees, blinking like some night creature caught in the lantern's beam. Alena *wouldn't* feel guilty to be starting back to school on such a wonderful, breezy day. She would only feel glad!

Faith was scooting across the bed to throw her arms around Alena's neck.

"A ride," she cried, climbing on Alena's back. "Gimme a ride to school, Sister!"

They had bathed in the tub in the kitchen just night

before last, so washing did not take long. Then Faith must be buttoned into her underthings.

"Hold still, Faithie!" Alena cried in exasperation as Faith wiggled and danced, eager to put on her new dress.

The dresses were laid out across the chair—dark green flannel for Alena, bright blue wool for Faith. This was one of the things Alena loved about autumn, the new dresses. They got two each year, the other at Eastertime.

"An' it's not a hand-me-down, is it, Sister?" Faith was saying as Alena slipped the blue dress over her head and began to button her up.

Again Alena was nudged by guilt. As the eldest, she never had hand-me-downs, but Faith got little else. Alena kissed the top of her sister's head.

"Come on, Faithie," she said. "Let's go out back."

The tantalizing smell of sausage frying greeted Alena when they came into the kitchen from the privy.

"Want me to mix up the pancakes, Mother?" she asked without even saying good morning. Her stomach was growling.

"Mornin,' Alena. Mornin', Faith," Mother said, kissing them as she passed from table to range.

Alena looked at her carefully, as she had done every morning since she had heard her parents talking. Mother's face looked white and puffy, and she moved clumsily beneath the full Mother Hubbard dress she wore, But, I don't think she looks any worse than last time, Alena thought, trying to remember how Mother had been last autumn before Samuel was born.

"You'd be most help doing up Faith's hair and your own," Mother was saying. "Then she and Fritz can feed the chickens and gather the eggs while you get the little boys up. It'll be a while before Father and William come in from the stock."

Alena groaned inwardly. So long to wait for breakfast! She had wakened starving, it seemed to her. Not even first-day-of-school nerves took *her* appetite.

By the time Father and ten-year-old William came in from milking, Alena, a green ribbon tied jauntily in her hair, was setting bowls of steaming mush and platters of corn cakes and fried eggs and sausage on the table. Faith, her braids tied up with blue, and eight-year-old Fritz were already at the table. Three-year-old Delbert was perched on a wooden grocery box on top of a chair, and baby Samuel was tied with a tea towel into the high chair. Mother brought the syrup pitcher and a crock of apple butter, and she and Alena sat down. They waited, the fragrant food before them making Alena's empty stomach roll, while Father and William washed up. Alena wished she could bang *her* spoon on the table as baby Samuel did.

At last Father and William were seated, and the grace

had been said. Alena dug her spoon eagerly into the buttery mush and reached for the sugar bowl with her other hand.

"Alena!" Father said, his eyebrows raised, and Alena felt the color rising in her cheeks even before William sang out, "What a greedy Gus Alena is!"

From the rolling fields on either side of the road, the clatter of machinery and the voices of men at work rose out of clouds of dust. Dust puffed beneath Alena's hurrying feet, too. Her shoes and stockings were getting dirty, she knew, but Alena didn't care. She wanted only to be away, as quickly as she could, from home's endless chores and Mother's tired face and Father's accusing eyes.

Alena yanked Faith along beside her. The boys were following. Alena glanced back and saw they had stopped at the corner of a split-rail fence. They were picking blackberries. She could see that Fritz's lips were already stained blue.

"Don't dawdle, Fritz. Will, come along," she called. "We'll be late."

"There's plenty time," said William, stuffing berries into his mouth.

Look who's greedy now, Alena thought, but she only said, "I'll tell Father if you're tardy."

At the crossroads, Alena's friend Violet was dancing

from foot to foot. Alena saw her wave when she caught sight of them. She came running.

"You'll never guess who's gonna be teacher this year!" Violet cried, linking her arm through Alena's and clanking their lunch pails together. Not waiting for a response, she peered at Faith, who was clutching Alena's other hand. "Hullo, Faithie. Goodness' sakes, you big enough for school?"

Faith drew herself up to her tallest and nodded emphatically, but Alena was suddenly aware of the nervousness of her tight-gripping hand.

"Of course she's big enough," she said to Violet in a warning tone. "She's already sounding out her words. School's gonna be easy for Faith."

Violet got the message. "Don't you think *I* know that?" she said. "I was only joshing."

Alena saw Faith grin as the three of them continued down the dusty road.

"Isn't Miss Guthrie gonna be there this year?" Alena said, remembering Violet's greeting.

"Nope," said Violet, clamping her lips and smiling mysteriously.

"Well, who then, Miss Smarty?"

"Miss Guthrie's gettin' married."

"No-o-o," said Alena. "Says who? I never heard tell she had a fella."

"Says Ma," Violet said. "Mrs. Streator told her, and

Mrs. Malcolm told *her,* and Mrs. Malcolm ought to know." Violet hugged Alena's arm.

"Violet Walt," Alena cried, "tell me this minute or I hope to die, I'll never speak to you again. *Why* ought Mrs. Malcolm to know? She don't even have younguns in school, unless . . . Wait!"

Faith was plucking at her sleeve.

"Are we gonna have a new teacher, Sister? Are we?"

"Any teacher'll be new to you. Now hush while I think." Alena wrinkled her forehead in concentration. "Unless . . ." She turned to Violet triumphantly. "Don't *tell* me Miss Guthrie is marryin' the *Malcolm* boy?"

Violet chortled. "Not hardly! My ma says he won't never marry iffen *his* ma can help it. No, it's some fella Miss Guthrie knew over in Peoria where she come from."

"Well, then, tell me! Who's gonna be teacher?"

Violet stopped in the middle of the road, dropping Alena's arm and facing her, flushed with the importance of her news. She drew a deep breath. "*That's* who!"

Alena stared at her, puzzled. Faith was yanking on her hand, jumping up and down and peering into their faces.

"Johnny Malcolm! Johnny Malcolm's gonna be teacher this year. Mrs. Malcolm told Mrs. Streator, and she weren't exactly pleased about it neither, Mrs. Streator told Ma. He was s'posed to be studyin' to be a preacher, except he come home this summer and said he weren't goin' back, and then Miss Guthrie told the school directors she was gettin' married, and Johnny heard tell of it, and now *he's* gonna teach the school hisself!"

They began walking again, Violet triumphant, Alena digesting the news.

"Who's Johnny Malcolm?" Faith was demanding. "Why can't I have Miss Guthrie?" Her voice was growing shrill, and Alena saw tears gathering in her eyes.

"Now look what you've done, Violet Walt!" Alena said. "Hush, Faith. Miss Guthrie's gone, like Violet said. Mr. Malcolm's the new teacher."

Violet set down her lunch pail and knelt in the dust in front of Faith. She gave her a hug. "Don't worry, Faithie. Mr. Malcolm . . . Don't that sound peculiar, callin' him *Mister*? Mr. Malcolm'll be a real good teacher. He used to *go* to our school when Alena and me was little like you. You've seen him at church, I'll wager. He's right handsome and knows an awful lot!"

Faith snuffled and wiped her nose on her sleeve before Alena could remind her of the handkerchief Mother had tucked into her pocket. "Is he nice?" she said doubtfully.

"Of course he's nice, Faithie," Alena said, wondering as she said it if it was true.

Violet straightened Faith's collar, and Alena smoothed her hair, tucking the curly wisps into the braided tails.

"If we don't hurry, we're gonna be tardy," Alena

said, snatching up her lunch pail and glancing back along the road where William and Fritz had come into sight, absorbed, it appeared, in a study of the ditch.

Johnny . . . Mr. Malcolm, she thought, hurrying along. She had hardly noticed him, it seemed to her now. Not like Violet, who seemed to know all about him. Well, at least having Johnny meant the teacher wouldn't be some grouchy old man or harebrained girl scarcely older than herself. Miss Guthrie, nice as she was, had not been very smart, Alena thought. Alena was always catching her in some mistake or other, and the big boys never did mind her and spent all day long causing trouble and making her cry. Maybe Johnny . . . *Mr.* Malcolm . . . *would* be a good teacher. She thought she remembered he'd always been at the head of his class.

"There he is," Violet was whispering, jerking on her arm.

Alena looked toward the schoolhouse. A young man stood, tall and slender, at the top of the steep schoolhouse steps. The morning sun glinted gold on his hair and on the large round watch he held in his hand.

Why, he's a man, Alena thought. A man full grown. And Violet was right. He *was* handsome. More than handsome. Alena stumbled on, suddenly oblivious of Violet and of Faith, clinging more tightly to her hand, and of the other children converging on the schoolyard. He's *beautiful*! she thought.

2

It Starts With a B

"GUESS WHO'S THE teacher!" Alena cried, banging through the screened kitchen door that afternoon. Faith was on her heels but pushed past her to run to Mother first.

But Mother was not standing at the stove as Alena had expected. She had not been out in the yard either—at the washtubs, still steaming and full of boiled clothes, or at the clotheslines where the sheets hung limp in the afternoon heat. Instead, Mother was sitting, as white and limp as the sheets, in the rocker by the window. Samuel was crawling on the floor at her feet, whimpering irritably.

"Why, Mother . . . ," Alena said, catching sight of her mother's still face and closed eyes.

The eyes flew open. Mother started up.

"My goodness! I didn't mean to . . . I only sat down for a moment . . ."

Faith clutched Mother around her bulging waist and

buried her face in Mother's apron, making her fall back into the chair.

"Why, Faith," said Mother, still blinking sleepily. "How did you like your first day of school?"

Mother's face was puffy and odd looking, Alena thought. And what was she doing asleep in the middle of wash day, with the laundry soaking in the yard—Alena realized the clothes should have been rinsed and on the lines long before this—and supper to be gotten soon?

"I didn't!" said Faith, her voice muffled in Mother's apron.

Mother put her hand under Faith's chin and lifted her face. "You didn't like school?" she said. "Why ever not?"

"Just didn't," said Faith.

"She was too wiggly, Mother," Alena said. "She wouldn't sit still, so Mr. Malcolm made her sit in the corner. Mr. Malcolm says we must learn to discipline our bodies, as well as our minds. He says—"

"Well, now, Faith," Mother said. "First days are always difficult. I'm sure tomorrow will be better."

Faith shook her head stubbornly. "Not going tomorrow," she said. "Don't like school."

Mother put her lips together. "We'll see," she said. "I imagine you're tired after such a long day. And hungry? How'd a piece of sugar bread taste?"

Faith hopped up, her eyes bright. "Sugar bread?"

"Alena . . . ," Mother said, heaving herself once more from the rocker. "Would you . . ."

And Alena, sighing because she, too, was tired and hungry, nodded and went to the pantry for the bread and sugar.

"Faith, you'll have to fetch the butter from the springhouse," Mother said. She bent to pick up Samuel. "Where are the boys?" she said to Alena, and then suddenly, "Good gracious, where is Delbert? He was right here in the kitchen with me . . . Alena, Faith, help me look for him! I can't have been asleep long. . . ."

Mother was running, in a lumbering sort of run, toward the back door. "The wash water . . . ," she was saying, her voice shrill. "I'd have heard if he'd gotten into the wash water, he'd have cried. . . ."

"He wasn't in the yard, Mother," Alena said, her heart in her throat. Where could a three-year-old get to so quick—if, as Mother had said, she hadn't been asleep long? "Maybe upstairs . . . ," she said, already turned toward the stairwell, and then she was stopped by an eager little voice from the woodbox.

"Sugar bread?" it was saying.

Alena whirled and saw Delbert's head appear over the edge.

"Me have sugar bread, too?" said Delbert.

Mother was holding on to the screen door as though to keep from falling. Alena saw her close her eyes for a moment.

"Delbert Ostermann!" Alena said. "You'll be the death of us all!"

Mother's voice was low and toneless. "I need to get that washing done, Alena," she was saying. "Can you take care of the children? I imagine Samuel's diaper needs changing, and put a tea towel round his neck before you give him his sugar bread—Delbert, too—and see Faith puts the butter back when you've finished with it. In this heat it's a puddle in minutes. And—"

"Yes, Mother," Alena said. "I'll take care of it, don't worry. I'll be out in a bit to help with the wash."

Mother's face flickered with a smile—as if someone had lit a candle behind her eyes, Alena thought—and suddenly Alena didn't feel so cross.

"Whatever would I do without you?" Mother said before she went out the door.

I'll tell her about Mr. Malcolm later, Alena thought.

"Scoot for the butter, Faithie," she said, picking up the knife to slice the bread.

But there was no opportunity to tell Mother about Mr. Malcolm that day. While Alena hung the clothes on the line, Mother was starting supper, and the kitchen was too full of commotion as Alena set the table and helped dish up. At supper, William and Fritz and Faith clamored to give their versions of the new teacher.

"He's awful strict, Father," said William.

"He talks peculiar," said Fritz, "all full of big words."

Beautiful words, and he keeps the classroom . . . serene, Alena thought.

"He's got a switch," said Faith.

Then Samuel overturned his dish, and Delbert fell off his grocery box, and all Alena was ever able to say in Mr. Malcolm's defense was, "Maybe *this* year the big boys won't *run* the school."

As she washed the dishes and William dried, Alena shaped her mouth silently to pronounce words in the refined way Mr. Malcolm did.

Pew-*pills,* instead of pew-*pulls.*

Abso-*lewt,* instead of abso-*loot.*

Si-*lence,* instead of si-*lunce.*

"*Pupils,*" he would say, "we will have *absolute silence* now, if you please."

When the little ones were in bed, Mother came out to the porch where Father had dragged their chairs to try to catch a breeze. She sank into the rocker and opened her basket of mending.

Now, thought Alena, moving to sit at her feet on the steps.

But Father was telling Mother about the threshing, how he'd be gone a week with the crew in trade for the machine's coming to thresh their oats. And then William was begging to go, too.

"I'm old enough, Father," he was saying. "I can help

with bandcutting as well as Clarence Hadley, and if they counted me half a man, it'd mean you wouldn't need to work so long."

"I know you're capable, Son," Father said, "but taking off school for threshing's apt to hurt your studies and . . ."

Father worries about *William's* studies, Alena thought bitterly, watching an ant painfully drag an irridescent fly's wing through the grass that grew by the steps.

". . . you're small for your age," Father was saying. "The pace is punishing . . ."

I wonder what she's going to use that wing for, Alena thought. It didn't look as though it contained much nourishment. Maybe it's a decoration for her parlor, Alena speculated, envisioning a little ant parlor somewhere in the subterranean passages of the anthill. The fly's wing could be hung on the wall the way Mrs. Walt's Chinese fan was hung in *her* best room. What else would an ant have in her parlor? A hair wreath made of the antennae of departed ant family-members? A shiny black beetle-shell sofa? A bowl made of red-spotted ladybug wings? It was difficult to think of things tiny enough . . .

"Well, all right," Father was saying. "We'll try you on bandcutting. Reckon you've got to start sometime, and it would be good if I could work it to come home sooner . . ."

Alena saw that this last had been said with a glance at Mother.

William's face was shining. He had his shoulders thrown back as though he were something, she thought. "What about me?" Fritz was whining. "I'm almost nine."

But Father's no was firm this time, and at last Alena saw a silence in which to tell the way Mr. Malcolm wore his hair in a pomaded pompadour. "It's all shiny and sleek and golden, Mother," Alena was saying when she realized that Mother's mending had slipped from her fingers, and her eyes had closed.

"Mother's worn to a frazzle," Father said. "Let her rest, Alena."

He rose and bent over Mother's chair, and Alena saw how gray his face seemed in the failing light.

"Mary," he said. "Mary, dear, let me help you up to bed."

The gentleness of his voice made a pain in Alena's heart.

Alena was in Mother's rocker on the porch, stitching her embroidery sampler. It was Sunday afternoon. Mother was lying down, and Father had taken the boys to see Mr. Hadley's new carriage team. Alena was enjoying the rare moment of solitude. The *tick* of needle piercing taut-stretched linen soothed her wandering mind.

She was thinking, of course, of Mr. Malcolm. Since she had first glimpsed him on the schoolhouse steps, she had thought of little else. And she found she could not call him Johnny, even in her thoughts, as Violet did so irreverently, giggling with the girls. Alena's Mr. Malcolm, handsome and manly, bore little resemblance to the gawky "big boy" she vaguely remembered from her first year in school.

No, Mr. Malcolm was a being apart, she thought. It was as though he had come from another world, a sacred world called College. His talk was so filled with knowledge, Alena felt she could listen to him forever—listen, her eyes drinking in his fine, mobile face as he read to them from the history book, from the geography, or most especially, always and always, listen as he read from the thick volume of Shakespeare he had brought with him from College. No other teacher had ever read Shakespeare to them. No other teacher . . .

"*Sis*-ter!" Faith said, and Alena started.

"Goodness, Faithie, don't sneak up on me like that!"

"Sister, when's Mother gonna wake up?"

Faith was standing in the doorway, her curly hair straggling from her braids, her pinafore soiled. Her smudgy face looked forlorn.

"In a bit," Alena said. "Mother's tired, Faithie. She needs to rest."

"She's *always* tired," said Faith. "I *want* her."

Alena let her sampler drop into her lap and held out her hand to Faith.

"What's the matter, Faithie," she said. "I thought you were playing with the baby."

"He fell asleep, too," said Faith, dragging across the porch to stand by Alena's chair. "Samuel's no fun anyways. He just knocks down my houses as fast as I build them and scatters the blocks all over so's *I* have to pick them up!"

"Well, the other boys'll be back soon, I expect," said Alena, absently patting her sister's arm.

Faith plumped down on the porch steps and cupped her chin in her hand.

Alena sighed. They had been nice, those few moments of aloneness, she thought, taking up her sampler again. But they never lasted long. There were too many in the family and most times, too much to be done.

"Is Samuel all right?" she asked Faith. "Where'd he fall asleep?"

"On the floor," said Faith. "I closed the door so's he can't get out if he wakes up. I 'spect we'll hear him bawling."

Alena smiled. "Good girl!"

Tick. Tick. Tick. Alena's needle went out and in, forming the tiny "lazy daisy" stitches she was practicing. The thread was just some old blue cotton, but when she had the stitches perfect, Mother would let her use the silks to embroider something beautiful—perhaps a pair of pillow slips or the border of a petticoat or a handkerchief or scarf. . . .

"Is it because of the surprise that Mother's always tired?" said Faith.

Alena blinked. "What surprise?" she said.

"Mother said in the autumn we shall have a surprise, and now it's autumn. School has been keepin' a whole week already, and it's threshin' time, and the trees are turnin', and Mother's gettin' tireder and tireder, and I just wondered, is it because of the surprise?" Faith's voice had risen plaintively, and by the end of her long speech, it was shrill. She lapsed again into glum silence, but now her eyes were fixed on Alena, waiting for an answer.

Alena looked down at her embroidery and carefully looped the thread around the point of the needle.

"Don't *you* know what the surprise is?" said Faith.

"Yes," said Alena. "I know."

"Is it that I won't have to go to school anymore?"

"No," said Alena. It is I who would have to stay out of school, she thought. "No, that's not it."

"Then, what?"

"I know it," said Alena, "but I can't tell."

The surprise, of course, was the new baby. But folks just didn't talk about babies before they were born. Especially not to children. Once or twice, Alena had come suddenly into a room full of gossiping women and heard a word or two before she was noticed and the subject changed. And sometimes, Alena and her friends had whispered together, speculating on the hows and whys of babies. Violet thought it must be something like cows and calves. Cows and women must grow their babies inside them, she said, because they got so big in their middles. But neither girl had ever been allowed to see a calving, and it was clear from the way the grown-ups got so stiff and embarrassed that it wasn't a subject for asking about. "I'm sure it isn't eggs like chickens," Adaline had once declared. "Babies are babies right off. No shells or anything!"

In a way, Alena thought now, Mother has told Faith more than she's told me. I only know because I heard them talking.

"*Sis*-ter!" Faith was whining.

"I just can't tell," said Alena.

Faith dug the toe of her high-topped shoe into a splintery place on the step. "Give me a hint, Alena!"

Alena pulled her needle through the taut linen.

"It starts with a *b*, but that's all I'll say," she said. "And I don't know for sure if it's what's making Mother tired, or not."

3

Mr. Malcolm

FATHER LEANED OUT of the saddle and touched Mother's cheek with one work-hardened hand. He was looking into Mother's eyes, Alena saw, and his voice was as soft as his touch.

"You're sure, Mary," he said, "that you'll be all right while I'm gone?"

Mother smiled up at him. "Don't be foolish, Clay. I'm fine. It's weeks yet. Besides, Alena's here to help."

"Me, too, Mother," Fritz said. "I can help while Father and William are gone."

"That's right, Son," Father said. "You're the man of the family for the next few days."

"For heaven's sake, Clay," Mother said. "You'd think you were going to China, not just over to the next township. I promise, I'll send for you if . . ."

There was a silence while Alena's parents looked at each other, and then Mother's eyes slid away.

"I'll send for you," she repeated. "Now, go on, you two. I need to get the children off to school."

But when Father and William had ridden away, to a chorus of good-byes and waving hands, Mother did not turn immediately to go into the house. She stood, leaning against a pillar of the porch, and watched until they were out of sight, and Alena stood with her, wondering why she had such an empty, scary feeling in the pit of her stomach. As Mother had said, they were only going to the next township, to work on Mr. Hartweg's threshing crew. They'd be back by Wednesday, or Thursday at the latest, to thresh their own oats. Three, four days at the most. . . .

"Moth-er!" Delbert was yelling. "Samuel's pullin' my hair!"

Alena saw that the two little boys were rolling in the dust at the foot of the steps.

"Stop it, you two!" Alena cried, running to them. "Mother's got enough to do without your silly ruckus!"

She pried Samuel's chubby fingers open, and Delbert pulled away, rubbing his head and snuffling.

"Boys, mind Sister now," Mother was saying as she turned to go into the house. "Alena, Faith, Fritz, don't forget your lunch pails. It's time to leave for school."

Alena separated the two little boys and set them to playing with Delbert's ball. Then she followed her mother into the house.

Mother was handing Faith's and Fritz's lunch pails to them.

"Do I *have* to go," Faith was whining as she did every morning.

"I *could* stay home today to help with the washing . . . ," Alena said, the words sticking in her throat.

Mother held out Alena's lunch pail. "That won't be necessary, dear," she said, smiling. "The little boys and I will be fine. The water's hotting right now, and I've already got the starch cooked. I'm feeling much better today than I did last Monday. You can help hang out when you come home."

Alena felt her heart thumping gladly, but she kept a worried look fixed on her face.

"If you're absolutely sure . . ." She said it the way Mr. Malcolm did—abso-*lewt*ly.

"I'm sure," said Mother. "Now go on with you."

Faith was kicking at a chair leg and swinging her lunch pail glumly.

"Let *me* stay home, Mother," she said. "I could help, honest I could."

Mother laughed. "That's real unselfish of you, Faith," she said. "But, thank you, no. Now, scat!"

At lunch recess, the bigger girls always claimed the place beneath the single black oak in the schoolhouse yard. They settled themselves, spreading their skirts decorously, and unpacked their lunches from lard pails and baskets and brown paper packets. The boys were gathered beside the toolshed, wolfing their food and choosing up sides for a game of town ball. Alena saw that the little children were already playing some sort of pull-away game, Faith right in their center. She probably hadn't eaten a bite, so wild was she to be released from the schoolroom. Alena sighed. Well, they had an hour. She'd see that Faith ate something before they were called back in.

"Don't Mr. Malcolm act dignified?" Adaline was saying with a giggle.

"Just like city folks," Violet agreed. "You'd sure never guess he come from here in Hancock County."

"I think he's stuck-up," said Minnie.

"I'd be stuck-up, too, if'n I was that good-lookin'," said Violet. "What about it, Alena. You think he's stuck-up?"

Alena felt the heat creep up her neck as the girls turned their eyes to her. She busied herself with cracking a boiled egg on the trunk of the oak and did not look up.

"Dunno," she said. "He's all right, I reckon."

"Well, it seems peculiar to me," said Minnie, "that he'd come to teach in the very same school he went to instead of finishin' out his college. I'll wager he got in some kind of trouble down there in Carthage and *had* to come home."

"My ma said bein' a preacher weren't *his* idea anyway," Violet said. "Said he hankered to be a perfessor or some such thing."

Alena breathed more easily, glad their attention had turned from her. She peeled her egg with shaking fingers and stole glances at Mr. Malcolm from the corners of her eyes. He was sitting on the schoolhouse steps, alone, eating his lunch.

A professor, she thought. A professor at a college far away from here. Yes, he would like that, but if what Violet was saying was true, his mother wouldn't like it one bit. She wanted him to stay near home and preach, as her father had done. Alena wondered if Mr. Malcolm knew they were talking about him. What was he thinking, gazing that way, his steely-blue eyes fixed, it seemed to her, on the road that led away from the school. She tried to follow his gaze, past the thicket of hard maples that flamed against the sky. . . .

" 'Lena," Violet was saying. " 'Lena Ostermann, you in there? I declare, you're the worst woolgatherer I ever did see."

Alena blinked and looked at Violet, trying to think what she might have asked, but etched in Alena's brain was the picture of Mr. Malcolm with his fair head turned toward the horizon.

Clang! Clang! Mr. Malcolm was ringing the bell that signaled the end of the lunch recess.

Gathering up the eggshells and greased paper and

bread crusts that Faith had left when she hastily gulped her lunch, Alena shook her head. Faith had not wanted to leave her game, even for so long as it took to eat, and Alena had had to insist. She wondered if Faith had taken time to go to the privy. Mr. Malcolm didn't like it when children asked to be excused to go out. He said that such "errands" should be done during regular recesses. It was part of the disciplining of the body and mind he was always talking about.

Alena liked the idea of discipline, the way the school day was disciplined—the same things done in the same ordered way. It was a comfort to Alena, this routine. It was tidy and reliable and . . .

"Miss Ostermann?" Mr. Malcolm spoke to her as she walked past him into the schoolroom.

Alena paused, startled. He had never spoken to her before, except to call for a recitation.

"Yes?"

"Could you stay a moment after school today, please?"

"Why . . . why, yes, of course."

What could he want? She had done nothing wrong, and he didn't sound angry. In fact, he was smiling. Smiling at *her*. He had never smiled at her before either.

After lunch was penmanship. Alena loved practicing in the copybooks provided. Her own copybook page was easily filled with a neat imitation of the example of Spencerian script at the top. She loved the graceful

curve and curl of the letters, which fitted exactly between the ruled lines.

But she could see the way Faith was struggling,
seated near the front with the other first-graders. Her
pen was gripped in her stubby fingers as though a moment's relaxation would allow it to escape, and her
tongue was clamped between her teeth. There was ink
on her fingers and—heaven knew how it got there—on
her nose. Alena imagined there must be blots and smears
on her copybook page.

Mr. Malcolm was pacing slowly between the desks,
his long, white-fingered hands clasped behind him.
Alena felt him pause behind her, looking over her shoulder. Her pen trembled an instant on the loop of an *L*,
but then she heard his satisfied murmur, and the pen
moved on confidently, letters flowing from its tip with
practiced ease. Her face was hot, and her breath came
in little gasps of pleasure. Mr. Malcolm moved on
toward the front of the room.

Alena was concentrating on the copying of the last
word, and trying to compose herself, when she heard the
sharp clicking of Mr. Malcolm's tongue. She glanced up
and saw with horror that he had stopped beside Faith's
desk. She saw his hand reach out and pluck Faith's
copybook off the desk.

"Faith Ostermann," he said, "this book is a disgrace."

Alena felt her face burn.

"I realize, Miss Faith," Mr. Malcolm said, "that you are very new in school, but I am beginning to think that you are entirely too young to attend classes. These are not Spencerian *A*'s you are making. These are chicken scratches!"

Alena saw that Faith's face was white, the tips of her ears flaming red. She was gritting her teeth and staring straight ahead. Alena knew she was fighting tears.

"You have been in school a week now," Mr. Malcolm said. "That should be long enough to master a simple *A*. Perhaps your sister will help you. *She* is a splendid penman."

Alena hunched her shoulders in embarrassment. But she could not help the thrill of pleasure she felt. "A splendid penman," he had called her. Why *was* Faith so stupid and clumsy? She couldn't remember that *she* had had any trouble with her handwriting when she began school. Of course, as Mr. Malcolm said, Faith was young. . . . And suddenly Alena was chilled. If Faith was sent home, Father would surely make *her* stay home, too. . . .

I *will* help her, Alena thought. I'll start tonight. I'll tell Mr. Malcolm after school.

The last desktop had banged shut. The last footstep had scrambled from the room. From the schoolyard, Alena could hear the shouts and laughter of the liberated children.

She had entrusted Faith to Fritz and sent them home with a message that she would soon follow.

"Are you in trouble, 'Lena?" Fritz had wanted to know. "Are you in trouble like Faithie?"

"Am not in trouble!" Faith had said, poking him.

"I don't think so," Alena had whispered. "Go along. I'll be home in a trice."

Now she sat quietly in her desk, her hands folded before her, and waited while Mr. Malcolm stacked his papers and books and arranged his pens and ruler and inkstand in a symmetrical pattern on the top of his desk. Her heart was pounding, but she didn't feel frightened. She was sure she wasn't frightened. After all, he *had* smiled at her. He *had* said she was a splendid penman . . .

"I asked you to stay for a few moments, Miss Ostermann, to discuss this essay," Mr. Malcolm said suddenly.

He tapped a paper on the desk before him and raised his eyes to look into hers. Alena was impaled on the blue intensity of that look.

"M-M-My essay?" she said, her breath caught in her throat.

"Yes, your essay."

She watched his lips move, and his words echoed and reechoed in her mind, but it was not until later, walking home, that she could take in their meaning.

"I have not been teaching long, as you know, Miss

Ostermann," Mr. Malcolm said, "but I think I may have to teach a good many more years before I find a student with so clear an understanding of the proper use of the English language. Although this is your first essay for me, I would like your permission to keep it, along with any others I may find worthy throughout the coming months, in order to build a file of your work to submit, at year's end, to the county school directors. I believe you would have a good chance of securing the Lindley Scholarship for Prairie Township. You may know that this award entitles its recipients to a four-year's course in any normal school in the state."

Normal school. Alena said those words over and over as she drifted home, dazed. It had never occurred to her to think of continuing her education after grade school. She knew she was fortunate to have come as far as she had. Many girls, and even boys, quit school as soon as they could write their names and read enough to spell out newspaper headlines and do a simple sum. After all, what did a *girl* need with education? She would only get married, and then, as Father said, what use would it be to her? But with normal school, it suddenly occurred to Alena, there were other things to do. She could teach, as Mr. Malcolm did. . . . It took her breath to think of herself so elevated. Or perhaps she could . . . Her imagination failed. She could *be* something, something *important*, she thought.

Alena stumbled in a rut and had to catch herself with

a few staggering steps. Her breath was coming quickly, her head spinning. Normal school! Mr. Malcolm had said she might get a scholarship. Alena knew Father would not pay for a girl to go to school. Education was expensive, and unless one was to be a preacher or a doctor or a lawyer or some such thing as that, it was likely a waste, Father thought. But if I had a scholarship . . . Alena's head reeled.

Wonderful, beautiful Mr. Malcolm! *He* thought she could do it. *He* thought she *should* do it. Because he says I'm a natural-born scholar, Alena thought. A natural-born scholar just like him. Just like Mr. Johnny Malcolm, who was the most . . . *splendid* person in the whole wide world!

❧ *4* ❧

Taken Sick
Before Her Time

"ALENA. ALENA!"

Alena woke up to Mother's breathless, urgent voice. "Alena, wake up!"

The lamp was shining in Alena's eyes, and she could smell its acrid kerosene smell. She blinked against the light.

"Wha . . . What is it?" she said, her tongue clumsy.

"Alena, dear, please wake up. I need you to help me," Mother was saying.

There was something wrong with Mother's voice. Something wrong with Mother, Alena thought, struggling up.

"Get out of bed quietly, dear. Don't wake Faith. And come . . . come to my room."

Mother turned away, and Alena saw her white-gowned figure retreat across the landing. Alena slipped from between the sheets and followed. Mother was walking slowly and heavily, feeling her way along the wall as though she were not carrying a light.

What time is it? Alena wondered. The house was dark except for the lurching light of Mother's lamp. Alena's throat felt tight with dread.

Mother sank down on the edge of her bed. She had set the lamp on the table, and by its light Alena could see that the bedclothes and Mother's nightdress were wet.

Mother couldn't have wet the bed, Alena thought, stifling a giggle that bubbled up nervously with the thought. Grown-ups didn't wet the bed. Was it raining through a leak in the roof—Alena realized at the same instant she thought it that there was no sound of rain— or had Mother spilled something . . .

"Alena, dear, come here." Mother was holding out her hands, and Alena could see that her face was white and strained, but she was smiling a reassuring smile. Her voice was forced calm.

"What's wrong, Mother?" Alena said, taking Mother's clammy hands.

"Don't be afraid, dear. I'm sorry to wake you, but . . . but I need your help. Please listen carefully and do exactly as I say. You can do that, can't you, dear? You won't be frightened, will you?"

Alena felt as though her heart had stopped beating. She was suddenly cold and stiff with fear.

"No, of course not," she said, wishing her voice didn't

sound so shaky. She mustn't let Mother see how scared she felt. "What do you want me to do?"

Mother smiled again, but suddenly the smile was ghastly, and Mother's teeth were biting into her lip, and her hands had tightened on Alena's so that Alena thought her bones would break.

"Mother!" Alena cried, forgetting to be calm, but Mother didn't seem to hear her. She had closed her eyes and was gripping Alena's hands, viselike. For a long moment she stayed like that. Then her eyes opened, and she was breathing in loud, gasping breaths. She let go of Alena's hands.

"I'm . . . sorry . . . dear . . . ," she said. She made a motion, a sort of "just-a-moment" sign.

Alena waited, rubbing her crushed hands. She scarcely breathed.

In a moment, Mother said, "Now, dear," her voice itself again. "I need for you to waken Fritz, Alena. I don't want him to see me like this. It would frighten him."

Alena nodded. No, Fritz couldn't see Mother so sick. That was clear.

"I need for him to ride over to Walt's. He's to ask Mrs. Walt to come right away. Tell her I've taken sick before my time. Do you understand that, dear? *I've taken sick before my time.*" Mother said it slowly, emphasizing each word.

"I understand," Alena said.

"And he's to ask Mr. Walt to go for the doctor and then"—Mother was breathing hard, as though talking were work for her—"then to go for Grandmother Ostermann or Aunt Louisa and . . . and your father, if he can find him. I think he'd be at Hartweg's still . . . in Rock Creek Township . . ."

"Yes," said Alena. "I will. I'll tell him."

Mother was gripping Alena's hands again. "And Alena, don't waken any of the others and don't frighten him, but tell him it's important . . ."

"Yes, yes," said Alena. "Don't worry, Mother. Don't worry . . ."

Suddenly she couldn't help it. She had to ask. "Mother, is it bad? Are you going to die?"

Mother drew her breath in sharply, and her voice sounded angry. "Of course not!" she said. "Most certainly not! I've just taken sick is all and need some help . . ." Her voice trailed off. "Oh, Alena, I'm sorry, dear. You shouldn't have to . . . but there's no help for it. Now go quickly and get Fritz on his way. Make him take a lantern . . ."

She was closing her eyes again, and Alena saw the way her body stiffened and arched as she gripped the bedclothes and clenched her teeth.

Alena whirled and ran from the room.

It was hard to rouse Fritz without waking the little boys. Alena wished that William had not gone with Father. Fritz looked so small and young in the candlelight as he clambered out of bed, his skinny legs sticking out from beneath his long nightshirt.

But once awake and made to understand in whispers, Alena was amazed at how grown-up he seemed. She helped him gather up his clothes and boots, and they felt their way down the stairs to the kitchen, where she found a lantern and lit it while he pulled on his pants and shirt.

"Can you saddle the mare by yourself?" she asked, and he gave her a withering look.

"Father said I was to be the man of the family," he said. "I reckon I can saddle an old horse I've helped saddle a hundred times. What do you think I am?"

"Yes, yes, of course. Now tell me what you're to tell the Walts."

"That Mother took sick . . ."

"Took sick before her time," Alena corrected.

"Took sick before her time," Fritz repeated. "What's wrong with her, Sister?"

Alena shook her head. "Just say it," she said. "What else?"

"And Mr. Walt's to go for the doctor, and Mrs. Walt's to come, and . . ."

"And then Mr. Walt's to go for Grandmother or Aunt Louisa and Father—"

"Over to Hartweg's in Rock Creek Township," Fritz finished.

"Good," Alena said.

Fritz had pulled on his boots and was hurrying to the door. "I'll be back in a trice," he said. "Tell Mother not to worry."

"The lantern," Alena said. "Mother said to take the lantern so's you won't lose your way. . . ."

Fritz grabbed the lantern from her hand, making the kerosene slosh.

His voice was indignant. "Criminy, Sister, I'm not a baby. I've been to Walt's time and again. . . ."

Alena grabbed his face with both her hands and planted a kiss on his forehead.

"I know. I'm sorry," she said. "Now, hurry!"

Fritz, startled, looked at her.

"She ain't terrible sick, is she, Sister?" he said, his voice suddenly young and faltering.

Alena couldn't meet his eyes.

"She said not to be scared," was all she could manage in answer.

She could feel Fritz's eyes on her, searching, for just a moment more. Then he slipped out the door.

Alena clung to the doorjamb, watching the lantern bob across the yard toward the stable. She should go back up to Mother, she knew, but she didn't. Instead she watched the light disappear into the stable, and then she stared at the place where she had seen it last. The stable was lit faintly from within by Fritz's lantern, but all the rest was dark, and only the starlight shone in the blackness of the sky, and only the trill of a vesper sparrow, wakened perhaps by Fritz in the stable, broke the stillness of the night.

Was it a long time or only a moment before the stable doors swung open, and Fritz, the lantern in his hand, led out the mare? Alena saw him set down his light on the granite mounting block, then climb up to heave himself into the saddle. He looked very small atop the tall, broad horse. Much too small, she thought, to be sent out alone into the night.

She lifted her hand and opened her mouth to call him back. But he had already leaned out of the saddle to grab the lantern by its bail. He waved it in the direction of the house and rode away.

5

No One Else

WHEN ALENA SHUT the door and came back into the kitchen, she could hear Mother's hoarse whisper from the top of the stairs.

"Has he gone, Alena?" Mother was saying.

"Yes, yes, he's gone."

Alena ran to the stairwell and looked up. Mother was leaning over the railing, a white shadow against the glow of light from her room.

"What else?" said Alena. "What else can I do?"

"Shhh!" said Mother, and Alena saw her sway and grip the stair rail and begin the sharp panting that told Alena she had been seized again by . . . by pain, Alena thought. Mother was hurting, hurting badly.

Alena started up the stairs, but Mother waved her back. "No," Mother said. "Water. Get some water hotting."

Alena turned and ran to obey.

Why, she wondered, why did Mother want hot water? Why was she hurting so? It had to do, of course, with the baby coming. Alena had guessed that the first instant she saw Mother standing over her with the lamp. But it was too soon! Mother had told Father when he was leaving that it was weeks yet. And why was she sick? Did a woman have to be sick to have a baby?

Always before, when a baby came, the children had been sent to Grandfather's house. Grandmother and one or two of the aunts and perhaps a neighbor lady would come one morning or evening to visit, and the children would be hustled into the wagon, and Mother would smile and wave as they drove away. When they came back in a day or two, there would be the new baby, nestled in her arms. Of course, Mother would need to rest in bed for a few days, and one of the aunts would stay to see to the housework. One by one, the children would be allowed to tiptoe into Mother's room to visit and see the baby. Mother would look tired but contented and easy. It had been that way last October when Samuel was born. Alena remembered thinking that having a baby must be hard work to wear Mother out so, but she had not known it hurt her. Alena could remember when Delbert was born, and Faith, too. It had never been like this.

Alena's hands were shaking so that the water sloshed onto the kitchen floor as she carried the full kettle to the stove. She had built up the fire before she went to the well, putting on lots of dry kindling to make it hot fast.

The house was silent except for the padding of her bare feet on the wet kitchen floor. She went to the stairwell to listen, then back to the kitchen to wipe up the spill.

Then there was nothing to do until the water was hot, so Alena went back to the stairs.

Silence.

Mother's door was closed. The stairwell was dark. Alena began to climb reluctantly. She did not want to go up to Mother, but she could not help herself. She had to see if Mother was all right.

Alena knocked softly on Mother's door. There was no answer, and in a panic, Alena twisted the handle and rushed in.

Mother was changing the bed. She had put on a clean nightdress, Alena saw. The wet one was crumpled into the corner by the commode with the wet sheets. Mother was intent on hauling a heavy sheet of something dark and shiny onto the bed.

Alena stepped forward and grabbed it to help. It was rubber. A rubber sheet? Alena had never seen it before.

Mother looked up when she felt Alena's help with the rubber sheet. She was breathing hard, but she managed a smile, and leaning heavily on the edge of the bed, she gestured toward a stack of clean linen on the chair.

Alena jumped to get it.

"I can make up the bed, Mother," she said. "You sit down and rest."

Again Mother smiled. She lifted her hand to push her hair away from her forehead. Alena saw her face was beaded with sweat.

"Good," she said. "Good girl."

Alena busied herself with the bed, smoothing and tucking the sheets and trying not to see the way Mother fell into the chair or how she gasped and gripped the chair seat with white-knuckled hands. When Alena picked up the spread, Mother said, "No, no need for that," and instructed her how to fold a heavy flannel sheet into several thicknesses and lay it on the bed crosswise between the sheets.

"Now," she said, "in the top drawer of the chest . . . are some things . . ."

Alena pulled open the drawer. Neatly folded in it were a stack of tiny gowns and diapers, strips of flannel and squares of muslin, towels, and some pieces of narrow silk braid. There was also a bottle labeled SWEET OIL, and out of their place in Mother's mending basket, Mother's sewing scissors. The gowns and diapers were for the baby, of course. Alena recognized them as ones that Samuel had worn when he was new. But what were the other things for? She lifted them out and put them on the table by the bed as Mother told her to.

Mother had stood up and was walking around the

room. She paused by the open window and breathed deeply. When she turned to speak again, Alena thought she seemed better.

"Now," she said, "we are ready."

"Won't you get into bed, Mother?" Alena said. "Wouldn't you feel better in bed?"

"No," said Mother. "Not yet, dear. But if you would like to go back to bed after you have brought up some warm water and perhaps something cool to drink . . ."

Alena nodded and retreated from the room.

Go back to bed? How *could* she go back to bed now?

It took two trips, walking slowly and climbing the stairs carefully to keep the pitchers from sloshing, to bring up the water, hot and cold.

Mother drank thirstily, but Alena saw how her hand trembled and how she set the tumbler down quickly and gripped the sides of the chair when the pain struck again.

"Mother, what can I do?" Alena begged, tears coming to her eyes in spite of herself. She dashed them away. Mother must not be concerned for *her* now.

Mother smiled weakly when the pain had passed. "Nothing . . . nothing, dear. When the doctor comes . . ."

Yes, of course. When the doctor came, he would bring something for the pain.

Alena went to the window and looked out at the blackness. She strained for the sound of buggy wheels or horses' hoofs, but she could hear nothing. Not even a sparrow's trill broke the stillness.

Mother was up walking again, back and forth, back and forth, from wardrobe to bed, from bed to wardrobe. "Go to bed, Alena," she said. "You've been a wonderful help, but there's nothing more to do until Mrs. Walt or the doctor or Grandmother comes."

Obediently, Alena went out of Mother's room to the landing. Mother was closing the door behind her, plunging the landing into darkness.

"Good-night, dear," she said. "Don't worry. I'll be fine soon."

But Alena did not go back to bed. Instead, she sat down on the top step and waited. She was wide-awake. She could not possibly go back to sleep. She sat and waited in the stuffy darkness. And she listened.

Back and forth, back and forth creaked Mother's footsteps. Alena listened to their rhythm and to those long minutes of silence when the rhythm was broken and Alena knew Mother was closing her eyes and holding tightly to the bedpost until the pain eased.

Why was it hurting her? Alena rocked her body in misery, almost feeling the pains herself. Did it always hurt, having a baby? If it did, why did Mother keep having them? She, Alena, would never have babies if *this* was what it meant.

The moments dragged on with Mother's dragging steps. How long had Alena been sitting here on the step, listening for the doctor's buggy, for Mrs. Walt's saddle horse, or Grandmother's wagon? Surely Fritz had had plenty of time to get to Walt's by now. By now Mr. Walt should be on his way for the doctor, and Mrs. Walt should have come. It was only a little more than a mile.

When Alena heard the cry, for a minute she could not understand that it was Mother's voice, crying in that strangled, inhuman way. Then Alena was on her feet and at the door, wrenching it open.

Mother lay across the bed, her face twisted so that it did not seem to be Mother's face at all, and the crying came from her lips, open so that Alena could see her clenched teeth.

Then Mother's eyes opened and stared wildly around the room, falling at last on Alena, who stood frozen in the open doorway.

"Help, 'Lena," Mother panted. "Help me."

Mother seemed to be trying to get between the sheets. Alena ran to help her, hauling and tugging at Mother's ungainly body and at the top sheet. She helped Mother to position her hips over the folded flannel as Mother instructed when the pain had subsided somewhat, and to pull Mother's nightdress up around her waist. Alena was shocked at the sight of the great white mound of Mother's belly, traced with blue veins, and at her bare thighs, and for a moment again she could not move. Then Mother was drawing up the sheet to cover herself, and Alena could think again.

Where *was* Mrs. Walt? Where was the doctor? Grandmother! Even grumpy Aunt Louisa! Where was *someone,
anyone* to help!

"Alena, I'm sorry," Mother said hoarsely. "You are
too young, but there's no one else . . ."

Alena nodded, feeling suddenly that her cheeks were
wet with tears. But Mother didn't seem to notice. She
was speaking urgently, holding on to Alena's arm so that
Alena could feel the sharp, biting pain of her fingers.

"I am having a baby, Alena," Mother said, "and you
will have to help me. Do you think you can do it?"

No! Alena thought. Not me. Not *me*!

"Y-Y-Yes," she said. "What should I do?"

"Tie another . . . sheet to the bedposts . . . one end
to . . . either post. I need something . . . to hold on to
. . . something to bear . . . down against. . . . Do you
understand?"

But Alena had already grabbed a sheet, glad for some-
thing to do. Something to make her feel less helpless.
She got the sheet tied in place just as another pain took
Mother and was astonished at the strength with which
Mother grasped it, pulling so that Alena thought surely
the sheet would rip, or the bedposts be pulled over.

Mother was trying to speak. "More . . . water . . . ,"
she said. "More fresh . . . warm . . . water. . . ."

Alena ran to the commode and saw that a stained rag
floated in the pinkish water.

Blood! Alena stared at it a moment in horror, then

snatched up the basin and the empty pitcher and hurried from the room as fast as she could without spilling.

On the back porch where Alena took the bloody water to fling it into the yard, it was just as black and still as it had been when Alena stepped out with Fritz earlier. Had no time at all passed then? It seemed to Alena hours since Mother had wakened her, but the night was not moving toward dawn. Time had stopped, had frozen at this dark moment while upstairs Mother struggled with the pain and the little children slept, undisturbed by her cries, and she, Alena, ran about filling pitchers and carrying them and being of no real use at all.

Alena was pouring water from the kettle into the pitcher when a long, anguished scream ripped the fabric of the night. This time, surely, the children would waken, she thought as she ran, stumbling, gasping, heart bursting in her throat, up the stairs. But the landing was silent, the children's doors shut, and Alena burst into the hot, kerosene-and-blood-smelling oasis of light that was Mother's room.

Mother's eyes were closed in a face as white and still as death, but she was not dead, Alena could see from the heaving of her chest and the trembling of her legs, drawn up beneath the blood-spattered sheet. Her panting filled the room.

Then Alena heard another sound—the weak, quivering cry of a baby.

6

Matilda Jane

IT WAS THE tiniest baby Alena had ever seen. It lay in the mess on the bloody sheet between Mother's legs, wet and smeary and purplish colored. Its face was wrinkled shut, except for its open mouth, and its arms and legs quivered. It mewed plaintively.

"Oh," said Alena. "Oh, my!"

Mother laughed softly, and Alena looked up at her, startled. Only a moment before, Mother's face had been gray with exhaustion, but now her eyes were shining, and her cheeks were pink. Mother struggled to half sit and bent forward to look at the baby. She wiped the baby's tight-shut eyes and nose and mewing mouth with her fingers.

"Isn't she beautiful, Alena?" Mother said, gazing at the baby.

Alena looked at them aghast. Whatever could Mother mean—"beautiful"? Alena had had no idea that newborn babies looked like this. No idea at all that having a baby was so messy and painful. She understood now why the rubber sheet, the folded flannel beneath Mother's hips—to catch this awful mess. The baby had come out of Mother's body! Alena could still scarcely believe the way it had happened. It had come out between her legs the way an egg came out of a chicken. Only Adaline was right. There was no shell. The baby came out already a baby, and an ugly, mucky baby indeed!

Mother was laughing again, looking at the baby and talking softly to it. Her voice sounded like velvet, Alena thought, soft and thick and shining.

"We're going to need that water to bathe her, Alena," she said, "but first we must cut the cord."

There was a thick, slimy cord growing from the baby's navel. Alena thought it was some kind of growth, still another sign that something was terribly wrong with this baby, but Mother was saying that all babies had them.

"There's nothing wrong with *this* baby," she was saying, her voice exultant, "except she came early and so is a little small."

Alena got the strips of silk braid as Mother directed her. Gingerly, she tied them tightly around the cord, one close to the baby's body and the other an inch or so away.

"Now just use my scissors," Mother said, "to cut

between the ties. It won't hurt her," she said when she saw Alena hesitate.

But Alena wasn't thinking about whether it hurt. She was trying to keep her rolling stomach in place. She felt sick!

When it was done, Mother pulled the baby up onto her chest, paying no attention to the way her nightdress was being soiled. She sank back down with the baby on her chest, looking weary and satisfied.

"You're breathing, you're crying, you're perfectly fine," she was crooning to the baby. "You're a beautiful, perfect girl."

Then Mother looked once more at Alena.

"The water now, Alena."

She had spilled the water again, Alena saw when she went back down to the kitchen. When Mother had screamed, she had dropped the kettle back onto the stovetop and splashed water across the floor. But the kettle was still hot. The fire had not died down.

It can't have been very long, Alena thought in wonder, glancing at the black kitchen windows. But it seemed years since she had begun to fill the pitcher.

Here in the kitchen, Alena's stomach settled. But her mind did not settle one bit. It still raced, round and round, horrified, shocked, astonished at the way Mother was behaving—as though the baby was . . . well, as a

baby should be. As Samuel and Delbert and Faith and
. . . yes, even, long ago, as Alena herself must have been.
A pink, soft, sweet-smelling baby with downy hair and
milky eyes.

Perhaps Mother was delirious. Alena looked out the
kitchen window in the vain hope she would see someone
coming. Someone who could help with poor Mother.

But there was no one. She had no choice but to go
back up to Mother's reeking, untidy, oven-hot room.
Alena picked up the full pitcher and headed doggedly
toward the stairs.

Alena poured hot water from the pitcher into the
basin of cool water on the table. She tested it with her
wrist to make sure it was not too warm. Then she wet
and wrung out the rag. Finally she took a deep breath
and sat down in the chair drawn up beside the table and
Mother's bed.

Mother leaned over and placed the tiny, slippery
baby in Alena's aproned lap. Alena felt her breath come
quickly. Her hands were shaking. She knew that at any
moment the baby would slip from her fingers and fall to
the floor. The baby *would* not be still, but weakly flailed
her arms and legs and continued to wail, her minute
chest heaving with each cry.

"You are doing wonderfully, Alena," Mother was
saying, her voice weary now. "As though you had
bathed a new baby sister every day of your life. Don't

worry. She won't break. You'll soon have her clean and dry and warm."

Alena dabbed at the baby with the wet rag.

"Scrub her hard, Alena," Mother said. "Make her squeaky-clean."

Alena rubbed the baby's head with the cloth, being careful of the soft place, just as Samuel had had when he was small. The baby's hair was dark and curly, like Faith's, Alena thought. She wiped the little forehead and the sealed-shut eyes. The baby's skin had a bluish cast, but little by little, as Alena worked the cloth over her face and neck, she seemed to be turning pink.

What a cunning button nose she had! And that trembling little chin! Alena held the delicate hands together in one of hers, as Mother told her to, and saw how the baby quieted when her arms were held close to her body. She was smeared with something white that reminded Alena of tallow. It was not easy to rub off, but as Alena removed it, she could see the fine hair that covered the little body. She counted the five miniature toes on each tiny foot, the curling, wrinkled fingers. When the baby was clean, she rubbed her all over with the sweet-scented oil.

Mother told her how to dress the stump of the cord with a square of oiled muslin and a flannel belly band, but Alena knew how to tie the diaper, though she had never folded one so small. Finally, with hands now sure and skillful, Alena pulled one of Samuel's gowns over the baby's head. She was lost in it, Alena thought, wondering that only a short while ago, the gowns had seemed so small.

She laid a soft, knitted shawl on the bed and put the baby on it. The baby's arms flung out, as though she were frightened at being put down, but Alena swiftly wrapped the shawl around her, and the baby settled. She hiccupped, and Alena found herself giggling at such a miniature hiccup.

Mother was holding out her arms, but suddenly Alena didn't want to give up the baby. She held her close.

"Shouldn't we get you washed first, Mother?" Alena said, and as Mother was nodding regretfully, they both heard the sound Alena had listened for for so long—the sound of horses' hoofs.

"Lord a mercy upon us!" said Mrs. Walt from the doorway. " 'Pears I got here too late."

"Just in time," said Mother.

Mrs. Walt was clucking her tongue as she bustled to the bed. "Well, my girl," she said to Mother, and it sounded peculiar to Alena to hear Mother called a girl, "well, what have you gone and done all alone like this?"

"I've had a baby girl, Permelia," said Mother, her voice almost gay. "But I didn't do it alone. I had Alena to help."

Alena could feel her face go pink. She drew aside the

shawl so Mrs. Walt could see the baby. Mrs. Walt leaned over to peer at her.

"Seems to be fit," said Mrs. Walt. "Got all her fingers and toes, does she?"

Alena nodded proudly.

"Well, she's a mite undersized, but that's no wonder for a child who couldn't wait her proper time," said Mrs. Walt. "Who bathed her already and fixed her so nice?"

"I did," said Alena.

"Fancy that. You've got more spunk than I give you credit for, Alena Ostermann. Now, Mary, what about the afterbirth? You still havin' pains?"

Suddenly, with Mrs. Walt taking command, Alena felt a twinge. She had wanted Mrs. Walt to come, had wanted a grown-up to see to this scary, bloody business, but now that Mrs. Walt was here, Alena felt . . . After all, it had been she, Alena, who had waited with Mother all through the birth pains, she who had first seen the new baby, who had tied and cut the cord and wiped Mother's face with cool water and bathed and dressed the baby. . . .

"What you gonna call her, Mary?" Mrs. Walt was saying from the other side of the bed where she was massaging Mother's stomach with sweet oil under the sheet.

"I think I'll leave that to Alena," Mother said. "This

night she's earned the privilege of naming her new sister."

"Well, Alena?" Mrs. Walt said.

Alena rocked the baby in her arms. The baby had ceased her crying and seemed to be asleep. One pale, curling fist rested against her round little cheek. Her eyelashes feathered the edges of her lavender eyelids. Why, she really *was* the most extraordinary baby, Alena thought. She needed an extraordinary name. A name that was strong and graceful and . . . splendid, Alena thought. A name that sang. . . .

"Alena?" said Mrs. Walt.

Alena looked up into Mother's eyes.

"Matilda," said Alena. "Matilda Jane."

7

The First Day

WHEN ALENA WOKE up that morning, for a moment she thought it must have been a dream. For one thing, the air was cool on her face and on the leg she had flung over the sheet. Yet the night she remembered had been close and hot with lamplight and sweat and . . . blood. That was the other thing. Alena remembered the mess of Mother's bed. It didn't seem possible here in the clean white sheets of her own.

Then Alena realized how strong the light was, streaming through the window. She had overslept herself! They would be late for school.

She rolled over to rouse Faith, but Faith's place in the bed was empty. Sleepyhead Faith was up before her and . . . from downstairs came the clatter of dishes, and voices, grown-up voices. . . . Who?

She thought she remembered Mrs. Walt. Yes, Mrs. Walt had come in the night after . . . yes, she had come after it was over, most of it, because Fritz had taken a shortcut and gotten lost, she said. I *knew* Fritz couldn't find his way alone, Alena thought, though, of course, he *had* found his way finally, and Mrs. Walt *had* come, leaving him to sleep the rest of the night at her house.

It was all flooding back. She remembered that Aunt Louisa had come next. Alena wished it had been Grandmother, but Grandmother had taken a fall just the day before, Mr. Walt reported, so he had gone for Aunt Louisa. Aunt Louisa had acted a good deal put out at having to ride over in the middle of the night, Alena remembered. Alena almost wished she hadn't.

Even the doctor had come at last, entirely too late.

But it had been she, Alena, who had seen Mother through the important part—the scary, bloody, hurting part, the wonderful, laughing, *exalted* part of the night. It had been she who had given the baby her name— Matilda Jane Ostermann. Of course, the baby was true. Alena had only to hold her arms in a cradling shape to know the feel of baby Matilda. . . .

Suddenly, Alena realized that one of the voices downstairs was Father's. He must have come home some time in the early morning after Mrs. Walt and Aunt Louisa, finishing with Mother, had found Alena asleep in Mother's chair and sent her off to bed.

Alena slipped from between the covers. She wanted to tell Father! And then she stopped, her nightdress half over her head. Aunt Louisa—that *was* unmistakably Aunt Louisa's sour voice joined with Father's in the kitchen—Aunt Louisa would already have told him. Told him and Faith and everybody. Told them all what was properly *Alena's* news.

Alena yanked off her nightdress and snatched up her clothes.

Still, she was thinking, Aunt Louisa hadn't *been there*, had she? Only Alena had been there with Mother when Matilda Jane was born.

Mother's door was tightly shut, but Alena could hear Samuel fussing in the boys' room. She opened their door to the sharp smell of urine. Samuel's diaper and gown were soaked, and Delbert had wet the bed. He was sitting happily in the wet sheets, playing with Fritz's rock collection.

"Delbert Ostermann!" Alena said. "Fritz'll have a conniption if he catches you with those!"

Why hadn't Aunt Louisa taken care of the little boys? Alena wondered with a sigh. If you didn't get Delbert up first thing and onto the chamber pot, he would wet the bed for certain. Mother always did that and changed Samuel and nursed him and set them playing with something they couldn't harm before she started breakfast. If Aunt Louisa was here to help, why wasn't she *helping*, instead of blabbing in the kitchen with Father?

Alena stripped off Delbert's nightgown and set him, futilely, on the pot. She gathered up the rocks and replaced them in Fritz's cigar treasure-box. Then she began to change Samuel, who had set up a howl. It was certainly different, changing this big, wriggling, noisy baby, from tying on the tiny diaper of her new baby sister, her sweet Matilda Jane.

Alena came downstairs carrying Samuel, heavy on her hip, and holding Delbert's hand. Father was sitting at the kitchen table, a mug of coffee before him. Just sitting there, so late in the morning! Aunt Louisa was at the range, dishing up oatmeal. Faith was standing in the doorway, her face all red.

"No buts about it," Aunt Louisa was saying. "Sit down and eat your mush. I'm very cross you disobeyed me. Shame, Faith Ellen, shame!"

What in the world had Faith done to get Aunt Louisa so riled? Alena wondered.

"Faithie, I wondered where you were," Alena said as she set Samuel in the high chair. "Are you ready for school?"

She could see that Faith was wearing a too-small dress, and her shoes were unbuttoned and wet from the grass. She must have been outside.

"No school today," said Father, and for a moment Alena felt anxious. Was this the end of school for her after all? Father looked at her, and his face softened. "Just today, 'Lena," he said. "I promised your mother you could finish school this year, and I aim to keep my word, but I reckoned you should sleep after being up most the night. We thought Faith had gone back to bed, too—"

"I saw the surprise that starts with *b*," said Faith eagerly, slipping into her chair as Aunt Louisa banged down her bowl.

"—but apparently Faith disobeyed your aunt Louisa, who told her it was too early to get up"—Father was looking sternly at Faith— "and ran off somewhere. She's in disgrace, it seems."

"But I saw—" said Faith.

"Eat your breakfast," said Aunt Louisa. "I don't want to hear another word."

She can't have seen the baby, Alena thought. "What did you see, Faithie?" she said.

"I saw—"

"I said, not another word, young lady," snapped Aunt Louisa. "Please do not address Faith Ellen, Alena. She has been told to eat her breakfast."

Alena saw Faith's head go down and her lip go out. Why was Aunt Louisa always so cross? she wondered. She wished Father would say something in Faith's defense, but he was silent, gazing into the coffee cup he held with both hands.

Alena boosted Delbert onto his grocery box and sat down at her own place, not offering to help Aunt Louisa with the dishing up. Delbert began poking Samuel under the table, making him giggle. Faith poked her oatmeal with her spoon. When Alena tasted the oatmeal, she found herself making a face to match Faith's disgusted one. The oatmeal wasn't as good as Mother made.

"I hear," said Father, his voice bemused, "you had quite a night, Alena."

Alena nodded. "Oh, Father, it was . . ." She couldn't think how to tell him and stopped in confusion. "When did you get home?" she said finally, blushing.

" 'Bout dawn," said Father. "I left William at Hart-weg's, and I'd best get back myself soon as I've seen to you all."

"We can manage," said Alena.

"It seems *you* can," said Father. "It certainly appears *you* can."

Alena felt her confusion melting at the pride in Father's voice.

"Have you seen—" she started to say, but Samuel upset his bowl and began to cry. Aunt Louisa rushed to the table, a rag in her hand, scolding again, and Samuel cried louder.

Alena gave Aunt Louisa a look and took Samuel out of the high chair.

"Perhaps you'll want to lie down awhile, Louisa," Father said quietly. "You haven't had much rest, coming so sudden the way you did to rescue us."

Rescue? Alena thought. Rescue!

Father drained his coffee cup.

"Now," he said. "Faithie, Delbert, Mother and I have a surprise for you. Let's go see." He took Samuel from Alena and held out his hand to Delbert.

"But they haven't finished," said Aunt Louisa.

"It'll wait, Louisa," Father said. "Coming, Faith? 'Lena?"

"But it's in the orchard," said Faith, scrambling off her chair.

"No, it's not, Faithie. The surprise is upstairs," Alena said.

"Upstairs?" said Faith, her face puzzled.

"Come on, Faithie, let's go see," Alena said over her shoulder as she hurried after Father.

"But Sister!" Faith was crying behind her.

"Shush!" said Aunt Louisa.

Father had opened wide the door to Mother's room. Alena saw that it was clean and tidy, the sheets and coverlet over Mother spotless. All the clutter of the night before was cleared away. A small bouquet of asters stood in a tumbler on the table. The sunlit air of the room was fresh.

Mother lay quiet. Her eyes were closed. In the curve of her arm lay the baby.

Faith pushed past them and ran to Mother's bedside.

Mother opened her eyes and smiled. She moved the shawl away from the baby's face.

Alena felt her own face stretching in a smile to match Mother's. She watched Faith as she stood on tiptoes to look.

Faith's eyes opened wide. Her mouth opened, too.

"Your new baby sister," said Mother.

"Oh!" said Faith.

"Oh!" said Delbert, climbing up on the bed beside Mother.

Father held Samuel down where he could see, too.

"Ooo," cooed Matilda, crinkling her nose and her tight-shut eyes. Her rosy mouth made a circle, just like Faith's.

Faith reached out one finger to touch her on the cheek.

"Did she come with the butterflies?" she said.

Alena blinked. It was not what she had expected her to say.

"The butterflies?" said Mother.

"What butterflies?" said Father.

"The butterflies on the Osage hedge. I found them this morning in the orchard. I found them by myself."

"The monarch butterflies?" said Father. "Have they come again to rest on our hedge?"

"It's the surprise," said Faith. "The surprise that starts with *b*, like Sister said."

Father and Mother looked at Alena questioningly.

"Not butterflies, silly," she said, embarrassed. "*B* stands for *baby*. Our surprise is a baby!"

Faith was growing red again. Alena could see her blue eyes shine with tears. "But . . . ," she said. "But . . ." Then Mother reached out and touched her on the arm.

"That's *two* surprises that start with *b*," Mother said. "Aren't the butterflies lovely? And aren't you fortunate to have seen them?"

"Me, too!" yelled Delbert.

Alena saw Faith look at Mother. A tear trembled on her eyelash. Then Faith looked at Father, who was nodding, smiling. Finally, she looked again at the baby.

"She's as good a surprise as the butterflies," Faith said, and Alena wanted to hug her, her heart was so full.

Matilda Jane was even more beautiful than Alena remembered. As they watched, her eyelashes fluttered, dark against her cheek. Then her eyes opened, as blue as the morning. As bright, Alena thought, as sun on butterfly wings.

They were gone. Alena's heart went out to Faith, whose face was blank with dismay.

"The whole hedge was covered," Faith said. "Covered like with a robe, 'Lena! It was all gold and black and shining!"

"They must have gone on south," Alena said, laying her hand on Faith's shoulder.

Delbert ran toward the hedge.

"Butterfly! Butterfly!" he shouted.

"No, Delbert, the butterflies are gone," Alena called after him. "Careful of the thorns!"

Delbert reached a cautious hand to touch the hedge. "Gone?" he said. "All gone?"

"I *did* see them," Faith said, kicking at a tussock of grass. "I really did see them."

"I know. I saw them once. Father says they come through every year, on their way to California. They go there 'cause it's warm in wintertime."

"Warm?" said Faith. "Warm in wintertime?"

"That's what Father says," Alena said, scarcely believing it herself. Then she remembered Mr. Malcolm's geography lesson last Friday. "A tropical clime, that's what it must be in California," she said. "That means it stays warm all year."

Delbert was bending to pick up something from the ground. He held it carefully in two pudgy fingers and trotted back to them.

"Butterfly," he said, satisfaction in his voice.

He was holding a black-and-orange butterfly by one wing.

"Oh!" said Faith, her face lighting up, and then, "Oh," when she saw how still it was in Delbert's fingers. "It's dead," she said.

Alena knelt to look at the butterfly Delbert held out.

"Look how beautiful it is, even dead," she said. "It must have been lovely, seeing the whole hedge covered with them."

Faith nodded, her face sad.

"They don't live long, Faithie," Alena said. "Butter-flies never live long. Probably this one was sick or too tired to go on."

"It's not fair," Faith said, reaching out a finger to stroke the butterfly's wing.

"Mine," said Delbert, snatching it back.

"You know what I think, Faith?" Alena said, taking her hand and Delbert's and beginning to lead them back toward the house. "I think it doesn't matter that but-terflies live such short lives. They are beautiful, and everyone loves them. I think, while they live, they are happy and free."

She looked at Faith's face to see if her words had made Faith feel better. She couldn't tell, but a moment later, Faith began to skip at her side and hum a small tune.

Alena picked up her steps, going as fast as she could hurry Delbert's short legs. She wanted to get back to see if there was anything she could do to help with Matilda Jane.

8

The Second Day

"VI'LET, VI'LET," FAITH called. "We've got a new baby, and I saw the butterflies!"

It was Wednesday, and Alena and Faith were meeting Violet at the crossroads on their way to school. For once, Fritz was not dawdling behind, but had run ahead. Hurrying, Alena thought, to boast to the boys of his ride to the Walts. To hear him tell it, *he* had been the hero of the night the baby was born.

"I know about the baby," Violet said, laughing. "Wasn't it *our* house Fritz came to, yelling to wake the dead, and my ma who went to your mother, and my pa who got the doctor? But what's this about butterflies?"

Violet linked arms with Alena and leaned close.

Faith began to chatter about butterflies and babies.

"They were all over the hedge, and I ran to tell, and Mother showed me our baby, who was really the surprise, but the butterflies start with *b*, too, and they went away, but Delbert found one, only it was dead . . ."

"Ma says the baby was born before she could get there, and only you was with your mother," Violet was whispering into Alena's ear. "What was it like, 'Lena? Tell. Do tell!"

Violet's voice and eyes were avid.

Alena pulled away a little, rolling her eyes significantly toward Faith. "Not now," she said.

"Then at recess," Violet said. "Oh, I can't *wait* to hear!"

"She's got bitsy little fingers and a bitsy little nose," Faith was babbling, "so I call her Bitsy, but her name is 'Tilda Jane. . . .'"

"Goodness' sakes, Faithie," said Violet. "I never heard you talk so much in all your life."

Alena felt relieved that Violet had stopped asking questions. How *could* she tell, after all? She didn't have the words, and even if she had, would Violet believe what had happened when even she, who had been there, could not believe it herself?

Mr. Malcolm was calling the roll.

"Ostermann, Alena."

"Present," Alena said.

Mr. Malcolm lifted his eyes from the roll book.

"So I see. Was your *entire* family working on a threshing crew yesterday, Miss Ostermann?"

Alena squirmed inwardly at the tone of his voice. He had seemed cross Monday when she told him that William was threshing with Father. Though what he took exception to, she couldn't imagine. Most of the older boys did not attend school at all until the harvest was done.

"No, sir," she said. "We . . . we have a new baby at our house, and Father kept us home yesterday because . . . because Fritz had to ride for help . . ."

From the corner of her eye, she could see Fritz sit up straighter in his desk. Several of the children turned to look at him.

". . . in the middle of the night, you see, and . . . and Faith's too little to come to school alone and . . ."

"I see," said Mr. Malcolm, his voice abrupt. "You may spare us the details, Miss Ostermann. However, you will need to see me at recess, you and Miss Faith and Master Fritz, for the work you have missed."

"Yes, sir," said Alena, feeling rebuked, though she did not know why. She looked at her desktop.

"Ostermann, Faith, Ostermann, Fritz, both present. Ostermann, William, still absent, I see," said Mr. Malcolm, checking off the names in his book. "Peachey, Amelia?"

"Prethent," lisped Amelia Peachey.

Alena had been dreading recess. First, of course, she and Fritz and Faith had to stay in. That had almost undone Faith, Alena thought. She could scarcely get to recess as it was without being reprimanded at least once for whispering or wiggling or woolgathering. And whenever Mr. Malcolm spoke to her, she got tongue-tied and clumsy and red in the face. So staying in had been the first ordeal.

Mr. Malcolm had not kept them long. He had been quick and cool, looking up the pages each should have studied and the problems each should have worked, and then he had dismissed them without further comment. He had not said anything more about normal school. Perhaps he had changed his mind about that, Alena thought. Perhaps he had remembered she was only a girl.

Now she must face Violet and try to tell her about the baby. Alena took a deep breath and followed Faith and Fritz, who had started running down the schoolhouse steps as soon as they were over the threshold.

" 'Lena," Violet called. "Over here!"

Alena was distressed to see that not only Violet was waiting for her under the oak, but Adaline Elford and Minnie Chalmers as well. Violet was gesturing enthusiastically.

Alena walked toward them slowly. She could feel herself blushing already. Her eyes darted sideways, looking for an excuse to escape, but none presented itself.

"H'lo," she said. "Whatcha doing?"

Violet giggled.

"Waiting for you, silly. Now tell us! We've been perishing to hear. Did you really see the baby get born?"

Alena sat down, taking time to arrange her skirts. She picked up a twig and twirled it in her fingers.

"Uh-huh," she said, not looking at the girls.

"Well?" Violet demanded.

"Well what?" said Alena.

"Well, what was it like?"

From beneath her eyelashes, Alena could see three pairs of wide-open eyes gazing at her intently. Violet's tongue was caught between her teeth.

"Kinda scary," Alena said.

"Scary?" said Violet.

"My mother says you can die having a baby," said Minnie.

"Does it hurt?" said Adaline.

Alena nodded. "But afterwards," she said, "afterwards it was . . ." She stopped. How to describe what it had been like to see that tiny living child where moments before had been no one? "She's a wonderful baby," Alena said. "I got to name her."

"Where did it come out?" said Adaline.

Again Alena dropped her eyes. "From between Mother's . . ."—it seemed so crude to say *legs*, Alena thought—"limbs," she said.

"I thought so!" said Adaline triumphantly. "And there wasn't any shell, was there?"

Alena shook her head.

"Told you," said Adaline.

Minnie and Violet were looking at Alena. She could see respect in their eyes.

"Did you swoon?" asked Violet.

"Wasn't time," said Alena.

"What were you doing?"

"Hotting water and helping get things ready and . . . afterwards I cut the cord."

The girls looked puzzled.

"They're born with a cord coming out of their stomachs," Alena said. "You have to cut it off."

"With a knife?" said Minnie.

"What's it made of?" said Violet.

"How'd you know what to do?" said Adaline.

"Mother told me . . ."

"She could talk?"

"Yes, of course. By then it wasn't hurting so much. And it's made of skin, I guess, or something, but it doesn't hurt the baby to cut it. Scissors," Alena said. "I used Mother's sewing scissors."

"But I still don't understand," said Violet. "How did it get out of your mother?"

Alena looked up and met Violet's eyes.

"I don't understand it either," she said. "She just came out. It doesn't seem possible. But she did."

As Alena helped Aunt Louisa with the supper dishes that evening, she could hear Matilda Jane crying. It was a weak, plaintive crying, and it had been going on for a long time—ever since Alena got home from school, all through supper, all through chores.

The floorboards above their heads creaked. Mother was walking her, Alena thought. Trying to get her to stop.

"Should Mother be out of bed?" she asked Aunt Louisa.

"No, she shouldn't be," snapped Aunt Louisa, "but she won't listen to *me*. Your mother, Alena Mary, has always been the *stubbornest* person alive. Even when we were girls, she never listened to me for all I'm the eldest."

"She is not either stubborn," Alena flared, giving the plate in her hand an extra-hard swipe with the flour-sacking towel. "She's just trying to get the baby to sleep."

Aunt Louisa rattled the pots in the dishpan. The soapy water sloshed.

"I *wish* your grandmother Ostermann were well enough to come. She might know better what to do," she said, and Alena realized with sudden fear that Aunt Louisa wasn't angry at Mother, only worried.

"Is there something *wrong* with Matilda Jane, Aunt Louisa?" Alena said.

Aunt Louisa pushed back a wisp of hair with the back of her soapy hand.

"Your mother thinks she's just colicky," she said, and something in her tone made Alena feel shaky inside.

"Should we send for the doctor, do you think?" Alena's voice was as shaky as her insides.

"If she isn't better by tomorrow, I think we should," Aunt Louisa said. "Yes, I think we should. She did come early. There could be something . . ."

She scrubbed hard at the pot in her hands.

Alena picked up another plate from the drainboard.

The crying went on and on. How did Matilda Jane, as little as she was, have the strength to cry so long? she wondered. The floorboards creaked.

Sometime in the night, Alena woke to silence.

Oh, good, she thought. Matilda Jane was sleeping.

She turned over and fitted herself around Faith's warm body. To the gentle in and out of Faith's breathing, she went back to sleep.

9

The Last Day

"I THINK, ALENA," said Aunt Louisa, "that you'd best stay home from school today."

Alena's heart stopped. She looked over Samuel's head—she had been tying him into his high chair when Aunt Louisa spoke—and saw that Aunt Louisa's back was turned. She could not see her face.

"Me, too," said Faith. "May I stay home, too?"

Aunt Louisa turned from the stove and brought a platter of corn cakes to the table, keeping her eyes downcast as she walked.

"No," said Aunt Louisa. "You and Fritz can go to school, but I need Alena today."

Alena felt herself getting angry. There was nothing wrong with Matilda Jane, she told herself. Aunt Louisa was making a tempest in a teacup over a colicky baby. All babies cried a lot at first. All babies . . .

"I can help," said Faith. "Let me stay home and help."

"You will go to school with your brother," said Aunt Louisa, her voice sharp, "and not another word!"

Mr. Malcolm was going to be angry that she was missing another day of school, Alena thought, watching as Faith subsided and glared at her plate.

"Father said I was to be the man of the family while he was gone," said Fritz.

"Well, it's women's work I need Alena for," said Aunt Louisa. "Your task today is to see Faith gets to school and back safely."

Alena saw Faith give Aunt Louisa a resentful look.

Fritz reached for the molasses.

"What . . . what do you need me for?" Alena said, and as she said it a thought struck her that took her breath away. She had not heard Matilda Jane crying for a long while, not since sometime in the night.

Aunt Louisa looked at her. "Just in case . . . ," she said, her voice trailing off, and Alena was even more distressed by the way she left her meaning unspoken.

Alena could scarcely eat. She had to chew and chew each mouthful. Swallowing was difficult, like swallowing stones. She strained to hear some sound from Mother's room. Finally, she put down her fork.

Aunt Louisa was feeding Samuel spoonfuls of mush.

"I can do that, Aunt Louisa," Alena said. "I'm finished."

"Why don't you go up to sit with your mother, Alena? See if she needs anything," Aunt Louisa said, wiping Samuel's mushy mouth with the spoon. "I'll be up soon as I get the children off to school."

Alena nodded and pushed back her chair. She felt heavy, as though all the stones she had swallowed for breakfast had lodged somewhere near her heart.

But going up the stairs, she heard something that made her heart lighten. The baby was crying again.

She knocked before pushing open the door. Mother was sitting in her rocker—Father had brought it upstairs while he was home—nursing the baby in her arms.

"Morning, Mother," Alena said. "Aunt Louisa wants to know if you need anything."

Mother looked up. Her eyes seemed to Alena unfocused. For a moment, Alena was not sure Mother knew her.

Then, "No . . . no, thank you. You can take away the tray," Mother said.

Alena carried Mother's breakfast tray to the head of the stairs and set it down. Then she went back in to Mother.

Mother's bed was all tumbled. Alena set about putting it to rights. As she smoothed and tucked the covers, she stole glances at Mother, and at Matilda Jane.

Despite the fact that Mother's body had shrunk back to something like its normal size, she looked worse than before the baby was born, Alena thought. Her hair straggled from its braid. Her skin was gray. Her eyes looked bruised.

Matilda Jane seemed to have shrunk, too. It was hard to tell, she was so swathed in shawls, but the dark head looked even smaller than Alena remembered, and the hand that poked from the shawls was like a bird's foot, delicate and clawlike.

Mother held her against her breast and guided her little mouth to the nipple again and again. Each time, Matilda Jane spit the nipple out. Alena could see that the skin of Mother's breast looked hard and shiny and swollen. Mother's milk dripped onto Matilda's face, but for some reason she would not suckle. She whimpered and turned her face away from the milk. Her fist trembled in the air. Alena could hear a sort of wheezing sound mixed with her cries.

"Hush, baby, hush," Mother crooned, her voice weary and monotonous. "Hush now, baby, drink. There's plenty of milk if you'll only drink."

Matilda's head turned from side to side. She cried.

Alena had finished the bed. She needed something else to do, so she took up Mother's silver-backed hairbrush and went to stand behind her. Mother did not seem to notice when she unplaited her hair and began to draw the brush through its thick brown strands, making it silky and smooth.

The stones had settled back around Alena's heart.

Aunt Louisa was carrying Samuel when she came upstairs.

"Now, Mary," she said briskly, "you have another

baby needs nursing. Let *me* have that one for a while."

"No," said Mother, clutching the small bundle to her chest. "No, she's not finished."

"She's not begun, Mary," Aunt Louisa said. "Let me try a little sugar water."

Mother's eyes looked wild, Alena thought. She had not loosened her grip on the baby.

Alena knelt in front of Mother.

"Mayn't *I* hold her for a minute, Mother?" she said.

Mother looked at Alena, and her face softened.

"Of course, dear," she said. "Hold up her head now, won't you?"

Gently, Alena took Matilda Jane from Mother's arms.

Aunt Louisa set Samuel on Mother's lap. He grabbed her breast with both hands and popped the nipple into his mouth. Noisily, he began to suckle.

Mother sighed and laid her head back against the chair. She settled Samuel into the crook of her arm and stroked his hair with her other hand.

"So tired," she murmured. "So tired."

"Of course you are tired, Mary," Aunt Louisa said. "You've scarcely slept a wink." She was beckoning to Alena and backing from the room.

Alena rose and followed her. Matilda Jane was a feather in her arms, a feather, a dry leaf, a bit of dandelion fluff. As light as . . . a butterfly, she thought, feeling the stony lump of her heart shatter as a picture came vividly to her mind. A picture of the butterfly Delbert had held out to her, limp and still, the morning Matilda Jane was born.

Aunt Louisa shut the door silently behind her.

"I've sent for the doctor," she whispered. "Mr. Walt stopped by early, and I asked him to go."

Alena nodded. "What's wrong with her?" she said, not knowing whether she was asking about Matilda Jane or Mother.

Aunt Louisa took the whimpering baby from Alena's arms. She shook her head.

"I don't know," she said. "Sometimes it's like this, and I don't know why. Mary's never lost a child. . . ."

She stood a moment, gazing down into the face of the baby. Seeing the look in her eyes, Alena suddenly remembered that Aunt Louisa had lost three children. Stillborn, folks called them.

"But Matilda Jane's not *dead*," Alena cried in an anguished whisper. "She's not going to die!"

Aunt Louisa shook her head again and started down the stairs.

"Bring the tray, Alena," she said.

Aunt Louisa tried dipping a clean rag in sugar water for the baby to suck. Matilda Jane turned away her face.

Mrs. Walt, who came at midmorning—"Charlie said the youngun was ailing," she told them—tried spoonfuls of bread sponge mixed with warm water. Matilda Jane turned away her face.

Aunt Louisa tried cow's milk and ewe's milk. "Perhaps it's Mary's milk that's the trouble," she said. Matilda Jane turned away her face.

When the sun was high in the sky, the doctor came. It hurt Alena to see him unwrap the baby so she flung out her arms and trembled and wailed. His big hands moved gently over her scrawny body. He pressed her belly. He looked in her mouth. He shook his head.

"Keep her warm," he said. "Wet her mouth from time to time with a little paregoric in boiled water."

"Should Mary keep trying to nurse her?" Aunt Louisa asked.

"Won't harm anything," the doctor said.

He went up to Mother. In a while, he came down again and drove away.

Mrs. Walt mixed up some bread dough, using the sponge she had brought for the baby. "No sense in letting it go to waste," she said.

Aunt Louisa set Alena to churning and told her to keep an eye on Samuel and Delbert.

Housework goes on, Alena thought, moving the churn paddle up and down. Through birth and sickness and . . . the work goes on.

Sometimes Mrs. Walt went up to sit with Mother. Sometimes Aunt Louisa went up. And once, at midafternoon, Aunt Louisa spelled Alena with the churning, and Alena went up.

Alena hated churning, but she would rather churn, she thought, than sit with Mother. Still, she didn't say so when Aunt Louisa said it was her turn. She just got up, stretched her aching arms, and climbed the stairs. She tried to talk to Mother, but Mother paid her no mind. Mother's whole self was intent on Matilda Jane, Alena thought. She sat hunched over her, rocking her, crooning to her, putting the nipple in her mouth again and again.

Matilda Jane fussed, but her fussing got weaker as the day went on. For long moments, she was quiet, her eyes squinched shut, her mouth open, her tiny chest heaving with wheezy breaths.

At one of these quiet times, Alena heard Fritz and Faith come home from school. She glanced at Mother and saw that Mother's head was leaned back, and her eyes were closed. Silently, Alena got up and tiptoed from the room.

"What did Mr. Malcolm say when you told him I had to stay home again?" Alena asked Fritz.

"Just gave me a mean look," Fritz said. He was munching on a warm slice of buttered bread Mrs. Walt had cut for him.

"Switched Fred Harrington today," Faith mumbled through a mouthful of bread.

"I'll wager he had cause," Alena defended. "That Fred Harrington don't know beans."

"Alena," said Aunt Louisa with a lifted eyebrow.

Alena looked down at her lap. "Did he read out loud today?" she asked.

"Dumb *Merchant of Venice,*" said Fritz.

"Just a bunch of big words," said Faith.

It wasn't fair, Alena thought. *They* didn't even appreciate what a privilege it was to listen to Mr. Malcolm's wonderful voice reading the Bard. The Bard of Avon, Mr. Malcolm had called him. . . .

"Louisa!" Mrs. Walt was calling from the top of the stairs. "Louisa, could you please come up?"

Alena sprang up. Something was wrong. She could tell from the way Mrs. Walt was keeping her voice calm and falsely natural-sounding.

Aunt Louisa put out her hand and touched Alena on the shoulder.

"Alena, dear, would you put away the bread and butter?" she said, and something in Alena's middle went hard and cold.

She had been feeling sorry for herself, while upstairs . . . Alena's hands shook as she put the bread in the bread box in the pantry. She sent Fritz to the springhouse with the butter. She wiped the crumbs from the table. She wiped the crumbs from Samuel's face. She gave him some wooden spoons to play with and sent Fritz and Faith to gather eggs. Delbert was building forts with the kindling, and she didn't stop him though he was making a mess. She wiped the drainboard. She swept the floor. And all the time she was listening for some sound from upstairs. Listening so hard that she couldn't imagine how she had missed hearing the horses and voices and footsteps outside. All she knew was that suddenly a shadow fell across the kitchen floor, and she looked up to see Father, standing in the doorway, blocking the afternoon sun.

"Father!" Alena cried, and the broom clattered to the floor, and Samuel, startled, started screaming, and Delbert's kindling fort fell down. But Alena took no notice. She ran to Father's arms and pressed her face against the rough cloth of his shirt. For a moment she felt his arms tight around her. Then he held her away from him and looked into her eyes.

"What's amiss?" he said, his voice tight.

"Ma . . . Matilda Jane!" Alena said, sobbing.

Father made a sound, low in his throat, and moved so swiftly toward the stairs that Alena could still feel the impress of his hands on her shoulders as she heard his boot strike the bottom step.

Alena sat on a kitchen chair, listening. Around her huddled the other children, William, Fritz, and Faith. They did not talk. Only Samuel babbled in his high chair, shaking his rattle and now and again dropping it so one of them would retrieve it, and Delbert made train noises, playing with some sticks of kindling wood.

When they heard the sound of footsteps on the stairs, their heads turned with one motion. Mrs. Walt came heavily down. She was dabbing at her eyes with a corner of her apron.

"Alena," she said. "They're awanting you, girl. You'd best go up."

Alena rose and did as she was told. One foot after the other, she climbed the stairs, thinking she had made this reluctant journey so often in the past few days that by now she should be accustomed. Did I ever go upstairs willingly? she wondered.

Father waited for her on the landing. He put his hand on her chin and tilted her face up to look into his.

"The baby passed away, 'Lena," he said. "She was not strong, and life was just too hard for her, I reckon. But now we need your help."

Alena was watching his lips because she could not bear to look into his eyes.

"Mother is taking it hard, 'Lena," he was saying. "We want her to go to bed to sleep, or she will be more ill than she is now. But she won't let us take the baby."

Alena nodded.

"Your aunt Louisa says you got her to give you the baby this morning. Do you suppose you could do it again—get her to give the baby to you, I mean?"

"But . . ." said Alena. The baby is dead, she thought. She nodded her head.

"That's my brave girl," said Father. He patted her awkwardly and opened the door to Mother's room.

Mother sat in the rocker. Back and forth, back and forth she rocked, the chair creaking softly. She held the small bundle of shawls fiercely to her breast.

Aunt Louisa knelt beside her chair. Alena could see that Aunt Louisa's face was wet. The tip of her nose was rosy. Her eyes were rimmed red.

"Please, Mary," Aunt Louisa was saying, a sob in her voice. "Please let us take her, Mary. There's nothing more you can do."

Mother looked past Aunt Louisa. She patted the bundle and rocked.

Alena felt Father's hand on her back. She glanced at him and saw he was urging her forward. She walked slowly across the room to Mother's chair and knelt.

"Mayn't *I* hold her for a minute, Mother?" she said.

Mother's eyes came to rest on Alena's face. For a moment she frowned, and then she smiled.

"Of course, dear," she said. "Hold up her head and don't wake her now. I've just gotten her to sleep."

Alena took the bundle from Mother's arms. It felt warm and light. She made herself look down at the little face.

Matilda Jane's eyes were closed, as they had been the first time Alena saw her. With a pain that took her breath away, Alena realized they would never open again.

10

Suffer the Little Children

ALENA WAS GLAD she did not have to prepare the baby for burial. Mrs. Walt and Aunt Louisa did that in the kitchen, shooing away the children, while out in the shed, Father hammered and sawed, making a little coffin of cherry wood. When it was finished, Aunt Louisa lined it with a piece of blue silk Grandmother sent over, and the baby was placed in it, on a feather pillow Mrs. Walt donated for the purpose. Then Father hammered shut the lid, for fear Mother would take the baby out again. She was acting *so* peculiar.

It rained on Sunday, the day of the funeral. The rain felt fitting to Alena.

After the regular Sunday service, Pastor Rost said a brief funeral service. Then many of the people drove away through the rain to their homes and Sunday dinner. But Alena and William and Fritz and Faith waited in the vestibule of the church with the aunts and cousins and Grandmother—who leaned heavily on Grandfa-

ther's arm and looked ill—while Father and the uncles
and Pastor Rost carried the little coffin out to the grave-
yard and put it into the muddy hole that had been
prepared for it. Mother should be here, Alena thought. If Mother
were here, Alena was sure she would not feel so hollow
and lonely. But Mother could not be out of bed, the
doctor said.

Alena shivered with the dampness. The rain went
drip, drip, drip from the eaves of the church, and
Grandmother and the aunts wiped their eyes with their
handkerchiefs.

" 'Suffer the little children to come unto me . . . for
of such is the kingdom of God,' " Pastor Rost had read
from the Bible, but that did not comfort Alena. Matilda
Jane had been such a special baby, Alena could understand God's wanting her. Still, it seemed selfish of Him.
We had her such a little time, she thought, remembering
how it had felt to hold her, all slippery, on her lap while
she gave her her first bath. It did seem God might have
spared her to them. He could have any baby He liked.
Why did He have to take theirs? Alena supposed she
was wicked to think such things, but she didn't care.
Matilda Jane had been specially *hers*. She could not
seem to forgive God for taking her.

The rain meant that muddy footprints were tracked
into the house, dirtying the floors Mrs. Walt and Aunt

Louisa had scrubbed in readiness for the funeral day. That made Aunt Louisa even crosser than usual, but Alena did not blame her. Alena felt cross, too. She had not cried since those few brief sobs in Father's arms the day Matilda died. She did not feel like crying. She felt like stamping her feet and shouting and throwing things against the wall.

But instead, she helped Aunt Louisa and Aunt Sarah and Aunt Veturia set out the food on the big dining-room table while, one or two at a time, the aunts and uncles went up to see Mother and then came down again, shaking their heads and whispering and looking at Alena and her brothers and sister with pitying eyes. Alena tried not to notice those looks. Grown-ups always made such a fuss about things. Mother would be better soon. Alena knew she would!

The cousins were all there. Cousin Emily, who had always been a trial to Alena, actually acted nice for once. But she didn't seem to know what to say, any more than Alena knew what to say or how to act at such a time. The younger cousins played and got underfoot as though it were any family gathering, and their mothers scolded and hugged them more fiercely than usual, Alena thought. She watched Faith and Fritz and William play hide-and-seek around the parlor chairs. How could they forget that the baby's coffin had sat on one of those chairs until this morning? she wondered.

Later she noticed Faith on the landing upstairs, just

outside Mother's door. Faith's face looked bleak as she stared at the tight-shut door. Alena went to her and hugged her, wordlessly. Faith hugged back, so hard it hurt.

The commotion of the full house made Alena's head ache. More than anything, she wished she could be by herself in some quiet place. But there wasn't a room in the house that wasn't filled with napping babies or playing cousins or men talking market prices and horseflesh and crops or women talking recipes and quilt patterns and croup. The only quiet place was Mother's room, and "Don't bother your mother, children," Aunt Louisa said.

The Walts drove over for the funeral supper.

"I'm awful sorry," Violet said, her eyes damp with sympathy.

Alena nodded, her throat too full to speak. But it made her feel a bit better, Violet's sympathy. She squeezed Violet's hand.

The table was heaped with food. All of the aunts had brought something, and many of the neighbors, too.

Why do they think we'll be hungry? Alena wondered. But the people did eat and eat and eat. Alena had no appetite at all.

At last, family by family, folks began to leave. The house had been filled for so long with people who did not belong there—ever since the night Mrs. Walt and Aunt Louisa came for Matilda's birth—that Alena wondered what it would feel like to be just themselves again. But Uncle John went home without Aunt Louisa. "I'll stay until Mary is on her feet," she said. Alena did not know whether to be sad or glad.

"I'll come over to help Louisa with the threshing dinner," Mrs. Walt told Father as she left. "Mary won't be fit for that."

Alena was startled. Threshing dinner? But yes, of course, it was time for the crew to come to thresh their grain, and they must be fed. It must all go on, in spite of what had happened—the farm work, the housework . . . Then, for the first time since Matilda had died, Alena's heart lightened. Schoolwork, too, must go on, she thought. On Monday, tomorrow, she could go back to school. To school and Mr. Malcolm.

Alena's eyes wandered away from the page again. She realized that she was searching the schoolroom for her brothers and sister, to make certain they were all right, as she had felt compelled to check on them over and over in the weeks since the funeral. Of course they were all right, she told herself. William was studying his geography, his forehead wrinkled in a frown as he memorized state capitals. Fritz was at the blackboard, copying sums with a nubbin of squealing chalk. Faith was reciting with the first-graders, her lips moving approximately with the others, though Alena could not pick out her voice as they chanted, "A fan for Ann. Can you fan me? I can fan you."

Alena bowed her head lower and found her place with her finger. What a deal of fuss over a fan, she thought. She had never realized before just how silly the *First McGuffey's Reader* was. For that matter, they all were silly. Certainly she didn't care a fig what some infidel Frenchman in her book thought of the scriptures. What she wondered was what Mr. Rousseau would have thought of "suffer the little children." Would he think it right that a little baby who never hurt anyone should die only three days old? Alena flipped the page impatiently. Why could her mind not settle to the lesson?

Then, suddenly, the words on the page before her were wringing her heart. This was not Rousseau, she saw, but William Cullen Bryant. And he knew! He knew just how she felt.

> *The melancholy days have come,*
> *The saddest of the year . . .*

Alena's throat was closed and aching again, and her eyes burned as she read.

> *And then I think of one, who in*
> *Her youthful beauty died,*
> *The fair meek blossom that grew up . . .*

But she hadn't! Matilda Jane had not had even that much life. She had had no chance to grow, no chance at all!

Alena closed the book with an angry thump. She was glaring blindly ahead of her when she realized that, all around her, the other pupils were shifting in their seats. She saw Violet's sympathetic look, even as she realized that the halting voices of the first-graders had been replaced by Mr. Malcolm's voice.

"Have you some difficulty with Monsieur Rousseau, Miss Ostermann?" he was saying.

Alena blushed and hurried to open her book again.

"No, sir, I'm sorry, sir," she said, fumbling to find the page.

There was a silence.

Then, "Very well. It is near dismissal time. Please put away your books, pupils. I will ring the bell in a moment."

Alena closed her book again, this time taking care to do it silently. She would take it home, she vowed, to study after supper. She could still feel the heat of her blush in her cheeks. What must Mr. Malcolm be thinking of his best pupil? His formerly best pupil, she corrected herself.

Since the baby was buried, over three weeks ago, Alena could not keep her mind on anything. At school, she found herself thinking of home. She worried about

Mother, who rarely came out of her room though the doctor had said she might be up. She fussed over the children—where were they? What were they doing? Were they safe? She wished Aunt Louisa, whose ways were so different from Mother's, would go home, and then wondered how, if she did go, they could possibly get on without her.

But at home, all she could think of was school. Mother was so strange, Father looked so gray, Aunt Louisa could not seem to manage the children, and they were so fractious that Alena found herself longing for school. At school she need be concerned for only herself. At school it was Mr. Malcolm who kept order and harmony. . . .

The bell rang. Mr. Malcolm stood in the doorway, ringing it. The schoolroom filled with the scuffle of children rising from their seats, the banging of desktops, the sudden babble of voices that was as suddenly quelled by Mr. Malcolm's voice commanding, "Order, pupils, order!"

Alena picked up her *McGuffey's* and her arithmetic book and unfolded herself from the too-small desk.

Violet slipped out beside her and took her arm.

"What about it, 'Lena?" she whispered. "D'you think you can come to the fair?"

Alena shook her head. "Dunno," she whispered back. "I'll ask."

They were passing Mr. Malcolm at the door, and Alena was startled when he put out his hand and touched her on the arm.

"Concentration, Miss Ostermann," he said. "Concentration!"

Alena could not meet his eyes. "Yes, sir," she mumbled.

Outside in the schoolyard, Violet pulled a long face.

"Concentration, Miss Ostermann," she said in a deep, precise voice. Then she began to giggle. "Egad, he thinks he's somebody!"

But Alena did not laugh. She knew Mr. Malcolm was right. She was not concentrating as she should. Her mind skittered and flittered. It would not light long anywhere. It made her tired.

"He's just trying to help, Vi," she said wearily, and Violet sobered.

"Cheer up, 'Lena," she said, squeezing Alena's arm. "Cheer up and come to the fair with us. Ma said your folks likely won't go, but I reckon they wouldn't mind if you went with us."

Alena nodded. "I'll ask," she said again.

Her eyes were searching the schoolyard and the road. Where were William and Fritz and Faith? Were they all right?

✺ 11 ✺

A Great Waste

ALENA OPENED THE front door softly and looked out on the porch for Father. Yes, he was there. She could see the glow of his pipe in the darkness and smell its sweet smell.

The younger children were settled in bed. Well, not settled exactly. Alena could hear Samuel fussing and Delbert talking to him. But she had helped Aunt Louisa get them undressed and tucked in. She had taken Faith to the privy before she went to bed. Faith was afraid to go by herself after dark, and dark had come early. Earlier and earlier each evening, Alena thought.

Aunt Louisa was mending in the sitting room, where William and Fritz were playing checkers, and Alena had been sitting with them, trying to concentrate on her lesson and waiting for Father to come in. But he had not come, so, finally, she had crept away to find him out here on the porch in the dark.

"Father," Alena said softly.

"Come on out, 'Lena," Father said.

Alena came out onto the porch and sat down beside him on the steps. She could feel his warm bulk in the darkness and hear the sound of his breathing. The smoke from his pipe encircled them both.

"I was going to come find you anyways, 'Lena," Father said, "to talk to you."

"I wanted to ask *you* something," Alena said.

She felt him nod.

"What is it?"

"Violet wants to know can I go to the county fair with her on Saturday."

Father puffed on his pipe.

"Do you want to go?" he said.

It seemed a peculiar question to Alena. She had not thought about it. She had simply told Violet that she would ask.

The fair. *Did* she want to go? She thought of the tumult of the sideshow with its fat lady and snake charmer and two-headed calf. She thought of all the visiting with folks, about quilts and canning and who won a blue ribbon and . . . They would all ask after Mother, she thought. She thought of breathing the dust of the trotting races and of stuffing herself with fried chicken and lemon meringue pie. She had always loved the fair, she thought. She always *had* . . .

"Not much, I reckon," Alena heard herself say, and

was startled to know it was true. "Don't feel like it much."

Again Father nodded.

"Well, 'Lena, if you want to go, I'll ask your aunt Louisa to stay one more day. Sure enough, you deserve a treat. You've been a good girl. . . ."

"Is Aunt Louisa going home?" Alena said.

"She's been with us 'most a month now. It's time she got back. Jack needs her, though they don't have younguns."

"But Mother . . ."

Alena didn't finish. She couldn't say out loud what she was thinking—that Mother wasn't getting any better. It seemed somehow disloyal.

"That's what I aim to talk to you about, 'Lena," Father said. "We can't keep your aunt Louisa any longer. It's not right. But Mother's still poorly. She can't manage by herself. . . ."

She doesn't manage at all, Alena thought. She just sits and rocks and stares. She never laughs or talks or even cries. But Alena didn't say it. Suddenly she knew what Father was going to say, and her heart went heavy and cold.

" 'Lena, I promised your mother you'd finish your schooling, but I don't know what else to do. There's no extra cash to hire help. Your aunts all have families of their own to care for, and your grandmother's not well.

You'll have to stay out of school for a while."

Father's voice sounded strange, Alena thought, strangled and low. Surely he wasn't going to cry? She put out her hand and touched him on the arm. She could feel the heavy drill of his coat and through it, the warmth of his skin.

"It's all right, Father," Alena lied. "I'm not much interested in school anymore."

Father leaned forward, his elbows on his thighs. He took the pipe from his mouth and knocked it hard against the heel of his hand. Then he blew into the bowl to dislodge the last bits of tobacco and shook them out. He straightened up and put his arm around Alena's shoulders and gave her a squeeze. Then he stood up.

"You're a good girl, 'Lena," Father said.

He walked rapidly away around the house in the direction of the barn.

Alena sat alone in the darkness on the porch steps. She waited to feel the disappointment she knew was there. But all she felt was the singing of the cricket frogs in the woods and the lingering scent of Father's pipe and the damp of the mist rising off the creek.

She was cold, she realized at last, cold clear through. She rose and went into the house.

"You got to tell him yourself, Sister," William had said. "He don't like it when someone lays out of school. It ain't fair he should get mad at us."

"He won't be mad," Alena had said. "I don't reckon he'll care one way or the other."

But she had been wrong. When she told Mr. Malcolm she was quitting school, he did get mad.

She told him at church on Sunday.

Mr. Malcolm sang in the choir. All through the service, Alena had watched him. Although she couldn't pick out his voice from the others, she knew that of them all, only Mr. Malcolm pronounced each word of the hymns clearly and correctly. She watched the way his lips shaped the words, the way his eyes followed along in the hymnal he held in his long-fingered hands, the way his Adam's apple bobbed above his stiff, high collar.

She didn't hear a word of the sermon. She only moved her lips in pantomime of the hymns. She was trying to find the words to tell him she wouldn't be coming to school for a while. For a while . . . That was what filled her with despair. Would she ever go back? she wondered.

When Pastor Rost said the benediction, Alena had no more idea what to say to Mr. Malcolm than she had when she took her seat that morning in the Ostermann pew. She stumbled to her feet and shepherded the children down the aisle after Father. Mother had been left at home, sitting by the window of her room in her dressing gown. "Mary, won't you get dressed and come to church with us?" Father had pleaded, and Mother had not even answered him.

Outside the church, the day was raw and cloudy.

The pastor and several of the ladies were asking after Mother. The aunts clustered around, fending off the well-meaning questions. Alena detached herself from the family group and watched the church doors for Mr. Malcolm.

Her heart lurched when she saw him. He had his hat in one hand. His mother, stout and resplendent in purple, clung to his arm. They walked past Alena before she could say a word. Mr. Malcolm's face was expressionless as he nodded to her. His mother was smiling and greeting friends, keeping tight hold of his arm.

Alena had to run a step or two after them, calling.

"Mr. Malcolm? Mr. Malcolm, please may I have a word with you?"

For a moment, she thought he didn't hear. Then he turned his head to look at her. He leaned down to say something to his mother—she stood only as tall as his shoulder—and disengaged her from his arm. She seemed to Alena to flutter and squawk for a moment—like a hen, Alena thought, her feathers all ruffled. Then she went on, stepping mincingly across the churchyard toward their buggy, her skirts held out of the dust with one gloved hand. Mr. Malcolm turned and came back to where Alena stood.

"Yes, Miss Ostermann?"

He was looking at her intently, his head bent toward her and cocked to one side.

Alena's head throbbed so that for a second she could not remember what she had to say to him. She felt as though she swam in the blue of his eyes.

"I . . . that is, my father . . . I mean . . . Mr. Malcolm, I shan't be able to come to school for a while," she faltered.

Mr. Malcolm looked at her blankly. Then she saw his eyes darken.

"For how long?" he said.

"I don't know." She could hear the edge to her voice. "Until my mother . . . I don't know."

He nodded once, abruptly.

"It is a great waste," he said.

Alena could not continue to meet his eyes. She studied the toes of her shoes. The leather was cracking on the right one, she saw, across the instep.

"I thank you for saying so," she said in a low voice.

The people ebbed and flowed around them. Alena was aware that they were directly in the path to the wagons, but she felt rooted to the ground. She thought someone spoke to Mr. Malcolm, but he did not answer. She could feel him looking at her. She twisted her hands.

"I could speak to your father," he said.

"Oh, no!" Her head came up, and she was looking into his eyes again, swallowing hard. He mustn't talk to

Father, she thought, not to Father, who had so many worries just now. "No," she said, "I really don't want to go on. I've enough schooling for a girl, I reckon. No, please don't say anything to Father."

He looked at her searchingly, and Alena felt his gaze burning into her face in a blush that rose redly from the neck of her dress.

"You are certain? Perhaps some arrangement could be made . . ."

"Yes, please." She could hear the desperate quaver in her voice and feel the threatening tears.

He looked at her a moment longer, and she saw that William had been right. Mr. Malcolm was angry, angrier than she had ever seen him, even when he thrashed an unruly boy. Why? she wondered. What did it matter to him?

"Very well," he said, his voice tight.

He turned on his heel and walked swiftly after his mother.

"Alena," someone was calling.

Alena turned blindly, the tears spilling over in a choking, miserable stream.

Violet took her arm. "Alena, what's amiss?"

Alena shook off Violet's hand. "Leave me be," she cried, sounding as angry as Mr. Malcolm had looked. "Just leave me be!"

12

Monday, Washing

"IT AIN'T FAIR I got to go to school and you don't!"
cried Faith, stamping her foot.

Got to go! Alena thought bitterly. "Don't say 'ain't,' "
she said.

Faith was glaring at her, and already, though breakfast was just finished, Alena felt cross and tired. She had
been at work since dawn, helping Father to fill the wash
boiler, chipping the soap, and cooking the starch for
laundry day.

"Get going," she said now. "The boys are waiting on
you. You'll be tardy."

"I don't care if I am tardy," said Faith. "I don't care
if I'm so tardy I miss the whole day."

Alena's hand shot out before she knew what she was
doing. She heard the resounding smack of it against
Faith's cheek. Her palm stinging, she watched the white
imprint of her fingers turn red on Faith's face. There
were tears in Faith's shocked eyes.

"Oh, Faith, Faithie, I'm sorry," Alena said, but Faith was gone. She had snatched up her lunch pail and run from the kitchen, out the slamming door.

Alena sank down into one of the rawhide-strung kitchen chairs. She put her head down into her arms on the table to shut out the memory of Faith's face. She could feel a sharp pain behind her eyes.

But a thump and a howl brought her jumping to her feet. Samuel had somehow slipped his tea-towel restraint and fallen from the high chair.

Alena snatched him up from the floor and felt him all over for hurts. "Oh, Sammy, Sammy," she was crying, but his howls had turned to hiccups as he stuck his thumb into his mouth. She rubbed her cheek against his and did not know if the wetness came from his tears or hers.

Alena glanced at the woodbox, filled the evening before by William and Fritz. She saw that Delbert was absorbed in his favorite pastime of playing with the kindling.

"Let's go up to see Mother," she said to Samuel. "Let's go see if she'll watch you while I get the washing started."

Mother's door was open. Alena knew that Father had taken to leaving it open in the hope that the family's activities would draw Mother from her room. But this morning, Mother was still in bed. Alena never got used to seeing her like this so late in the morning. Before

Matilda Jane was born, she had never known Mother to be abed when the children were up—not unless there was a brand-new baby, or that once when she had had the fever.

"Mother," Alena said, knocking on the doorjamb.

Mother did not answer or turn her head, but Alena could see that her eyes were open and staring at the ceiling.

"Mother, Samuel needs nursing," Alena said.

This one need was the only thing Mother responded to now. Alena saw her shift a little, and the straw-tick made a rustling sound.

Samuel was whimpering. Alena set him on the bed and walked around it. She put her hand on Mother's shoulder.

"Mother, Samuel needs nursing," she said again, more loudly. "Mother! Mother, you've got to nurse the baby!"

Suddenly she realized she was shaking Mother's shoulder harder than she meant to. Her voice was too loud. She snatched her hand away.

"I heard you," Mother said tonelessly. She was sitting up, slowly, reaching for her dressing gown.

Alena helped her into it. Samuel was crying now. Mother made soothing sounds, deep in her throat. She picked him up and carried him to the rocker. Alena saw that Mother's face was fierce with concentration as she put him to her breast.

Alena turned away from them and began to strip the sheets from the bed to wash.

Monday, wash day, she was saying to herself, trying to calm the angry beating of her heart. Father had gone out to the fields right after breakfast. The children were gone to school. What she had to do now was the wash. She would think about that, she told herself firmly. Only that.

Monday, washing. Tuesday, ironing. Wednesday, baking. Thursday, churning. Friday, housecleaning. Saturday, cooking for Sunday, and baths. Sunday, church and the opportunity to watch Mr. Malcolm singing in the choir and to talk with Violet a little, though it was difficult not to be snappish with Violet, Alena envied her so. Sometimes, of a Sunday afternoon, Alena took a walk or read if she was not so tired she fell asleep over her book. And then Monday, it all began again. This was the shape of Alena's life now.

As the weather turned rainy, the washing had to be done indoors and dried on lines strung around the stove. Sometimes it was late at night before the beds could be made up, with sheets still slightly damp, and Alena could crawl between them, numb with fatigue and chilled to her aching bones.

But in late October came an Indian summer. For two Mondays in a row, Alena was able to hang out the wash, and it was on the second of these, a cool and sunny

November afternoon with a sheet-snapping breeze perfect for drying, that she suddenly remembered the birthdays. She had been gazing at the yellow cottonwoods that grew by the creek, and at the thickets of sumac, orange, scarlet, and wine with coming winter, when she realized how late in the fall it was. Her arms, which had been lifted high to pin one of Father's shirts to the line, dropped heavily to her sides. William's eleventh and Samuel's first birthdays had come and gone in early October, she realized with a sinking heart, and no one had taken any notice. Always before, Mother had made wonderful celebrations for the children's birthdays with big fancy cakes and candles to blow out for luck.

But now Mother was . . . was what? Alena wondered. Not sick, for she had no fever or nausea or pain. Not— Alena did not like to think the word, and yet there it was in her mind—not *crazy* surely, for, though she would not accept the baby's death, she did not rant or talk to herself or see things that weren't there. Not sad only, for they all were sad, and they did not act like Mother. No, it was more as though Mother simply was not *there.* Only her body was there, rocking by the window with Samuel in her arms or wandering the house, picking up one thing or another and then setting it down again. Sometimes Mother would start a task—a bit of mending, or stirring a pot, or dusting the sitting room—but the first thing Alena knew, she would be staring sightlessly at a wall, the work forgotten and left half-done.

No, the forgotten birthdays were not Mother's fault, Alena thought. Mother was not really *there* to remember anymore. She had gone someplace away from them and could not seem to find her way back. Alena wondered if she wanted to.

Now Alena sighed and wiped her face with her sleeve. She bent to the laundry basket and took up another shirt to pin to the line. It was *her* duty now to do what once Mother had done, she thought. Father and the children depended on her.

For a moment the thought was heavy in her mind, and then she thought how good a cake would taste and how good it would be to see the children smile. If she could get the wash hung out before Samuel and Delbert awoke from their naps, there *might* be time to stir up a cake. A late surprise for William and Samuel. She began to plan what she could use for icing—butter and brown sugar and a little cream beaten smooth—and her fingers flew, pinning the wash to the line.

All through supper, Alena felt herself smiling. She thought Father looked at her strangely once or twice and realized that she hadn't smiled much lately. Indeed, none of them had. Meals now were generally silent affairs, with Samuel and Delbert providing the only noise, and that most often whining and cranky.

But tonight Alena kept thinking of the birthday cake,

hidden in the pantry under an overturned bowl. It had turned out well, she thought. Perhaps the layers were a little crooked, but she had beaten the batter so fluffy—it had felt good, that beating, the wooden spoon thumping hard and steady against the crockery bowl— and she had gauged the temperature of the oven so nicely that the cake had risen light and high and browned to a golden turn. Alena found herself wriggling like Faith on her chair, impatient for supper to be ended.

"Won't you have a little cold chicken, Mary," Father was urging. But Mother just stared at her plate, picking at a mound of tomato preserves with her fork.

Alena glanced around the table and saw that, except for Samuel, who was sucking on a bread crust, the children had finished their food. Delbert's head was on the table, his eyes closed fast in sleep.

"William," said Father, his voice tired, "you'd best carry Delbert straight up to bed. Then I reckon you've got chores to do and lessons to finish, you and Fritz and Faith."

"Father," said Alena, finding that her voice trembled with excitement. "Father, could you all wait just a moment? I have a surprise."

She saw the older children look at her, three pairs of bright, startled eyes.

"A s'prise?" said Faith.

Samuel banged his spoon suddenly on the table, as

though to herald an announcement, and Alena laughed.

"Yes, a surprise, if you'll just wait." She shoved back her chair. "Faith and Fritz," she said, "would you clear the table?"

Father was looking at her. She saw how the children's eyes turned to him and saw him nod. "Do as Sister says," he said.

William started to get up with them to clear the plates.

"Not William," said Alena, surpressing a grin.

"Not William, apparently," Father confirmed, and William sat back down, looking puzzled.

In the pantry, Alena lifted off the bowl. The top layer of the cake had slid a little more. Using two table knives, Alena straightened it as best she could and smoothed the brown-sugar icing. She poked two candles into the top, a taller one for William, a short one for Samuel, and arranged a few blue gentian blossoms on the plate around the base of the cake. She struck a match and lit the candles. Then, pushing open the door with her foot, she carried the cake into the dusk-dim dining room.

She heard the in-drawing of their breaths, the astonished "Oh!" as they saw what she carried before her, but her eyes were on the birthday cake, shining in her hands. She walked slowly so the draft would not blow out the candles, feeling her way with her feet. She did not look up until she had set the cake on the table in front of William.

"Happy birthday, William!" she cried, stepping back. "Happy birthday, Samuel!"

She saw that the whole family was gazing at the cake. William's eyes were round and glistening.

His voice was husky as he said, "But . . . but it's not my birthday today."

"No," said Alena. "I'm sorry, but that doesn't mean we can't celebrate. We never did say happy birthday to you and to Samuel, and this year was *his* very first."

Samuel was leaning from his high chair, reaching toward the candle flame. He crowed with delight.

"Happy birthday, William," Father said, but he was looking at Alena, his eyes shining. "Happy birthday, Samuel." Then the others were chiming in. "Happy birthday, happy birthday, happy birthday!"

Delbert lifted his head sleepily from the table and rubbed his eyes. Then he saw the cake and laughed out loud.

"Cake!" he cried. "Me have cake, too!"

Alena glanced at Mother, who sat quietly at her end of the table. She looked vague and confused, but she was smiling sadly.

"William," she murmured. "William and Samuel."

"Make a wish," cried Faith, clapping her hands.

"Yes, yes, make a wish!"

William looked at Mother, and Alena knew what his wish would be. Then he closed his eyes a moment.

"Which candle's mine?" he said, opening them again.

"The tall one," said Alena, "but you'd best blow out both. Samuel'd only drool on the cake."

They laughed as though she had said something funny, and Alena felt her chest expanding with the laughter. She ran to the sitting-room door and slid it open. Then, running to the pump organ, she plumped down on the stool and in the dimness squinted at the stops, pulled out two or three, and began to pump madly.

"For they are jolly good fellows, for they are jolly good fellows," she played and sang, her fingers feeling their way over the keys. From the dining room, she heard Father's deep voice, and then those of the children, join in. "For they are jolly good fellows, that no one can deny!"

13

Ironing, Baking, Churning, Cleaning

THE DAY OF the late birthday party was the last fair day of autumn. After that, the weather turned sleety, and looking up from her ironing on the Tuesday before Thanksgiving, Alena saw the first hesitant flakes of snow.

Mother sat in her rocker, brought downstairs to the warm kitchen. Her knitting was in her lap, but her hands lay idle. The two little boys played at her feet with balls of yarn. Alena could see they were unwinding the balls, making a bright tangle on the floor, but she did not stop them. They were busy and quiet for the moment. She would rewind the yarn later, when they were in bed.

"Look, Mother, it's snowing," she said, but Mother didn't answer. Instead, Delbert got up and trotted to the window. He stood on tiptoe to peer out into the frozen yard.

"Snow," he said, laughing and putting his fingers against the windowpane, as though to touch the flakes.

Alena put her cooling sadiron on the stove and picked up another, a hot one, with the quilted iron-holder. If the snow continued, Father might have to put the runners on the wagon for the trip to Grandfather's house on Thanksgiving Day, she thought. Everyone would be there. All the family. The thought made a fluttering in Alena's stomach. Although one or the other of the aunts often ran in to see what might be done to help them, the responsibility for the house and children was Alena's now. She wanted them to think well of the way she was managing.

Alena licked her forefinger and touched the iron's bottom quickly. It made the proper hissing sound, so she turned back to the ironing board, balanced between two chairbacks and spread with Faith's good dress. She was pressing their best things for the holiday, their newest dresses for her and Faith and kilt dresses for Delbert and Samuel. Samuel's had patches on the front where, crawling, he had worn holes in the hem, but that couldn't be helped, she thought. When she had finished the dresses, she would iron clean, starched shirts for William and Fritz and Father and make certain Mother's best brown wool was brushed and pressed. No one would be able to say they were not clean and tidy, not if she could help it, Alena thought.

* * *

On Thanksgiving Day, Alena did her best to do up Mother's hair in the way she had used to wear it. It was like fixing the hair of the French fashion doll Alena had seen in Cochran's store window last Christmas. Mother sat motionless before the mirror and looked at herself as though she were seeing someone else.

It shocked Alena to see how loosely Mother's dress hung from her shoulders, but she realized when she put on her own dress that she, too, was thinner than she had been. Her own cooking just didn't seem to taste as good as Mother's, she thought. No one accused her of being greedy now.

At Grandfather's, the aunts all exclaimed how well Mother looked, but Alena could see the falseness in their eyes.

Grandmother was still frail. She took Mother's thin hand in her own and patted it sadly. Mother did not seem to be aware. Grandmother looked past her at Alena.

"You were a good little helper when you were a bit of a thing, Alena," she said. "Now you are a stay and a comfort to your father."

Alena looked down at the floor. She could feel herself blushing.

"Mother will be better soon," she said, and all of the aunts nodded brightly and said too loudly, "Of course, she will!"

The aunts shooed Alena from the kitchen.

"Today, you go play," they said.

But the games of the younger cousins seemed suddenly silly to Alena, and Cousin Emily, over her fit of niceness on the baby's funeral day, was as affected and hateful as ever.

Alena spent most of the day in a corner of the parlor sofa, reading *Scottish Chiefs,* a book she found in the bookcase. Before dinner, the twitter of the aunts' voices from the kitchen made a background for the chiefs' battles, and afterward, their adventures were punctuated by the snores of the uncles, napping in their chairs.

Dinner was wonderful—roast beef and horseradish, plates of fried chicken, fragrant light rolls and strawberry jam, sour and sweet cucumber pickles, and apple pies and custard. For once, Alena ate until her stomach hurt.

With the cold weather, Father was indoors a good deal more. He helped Alena with the heavier work, but at many of the household tasks, he was clumsier than she was.

When her thirteenth birthday fell on a Thursday in December, Father did the churning for her, and Alena had a holiday, visiting with Violet, who was invited for supper. Violet brought a cake her mother had made.

*   *   *

On the Wednesday before Christmas, Alena baked some special things while the bread loaves were rising—gingerbread cookies in the shape of men and Mother's raisin pie. The whole house was filled with good smells. Even in bed that night, snuggled against Faith beneath the quilts with only her nose bared to the icy air, Alena could smell the Christmas baking, the gingery, fruity, cinnamon smell that she had created herself.

Father had sniffed the smell appreciatively when he came in that afternoon.

"Smells like Christmas," he had said, his eyes crinkling in a soft, rare smile. "You *are* a good girl, Alena."

The very next day, Father went to the village and returned with an armload of packages tied up mysteriously with string.

Could Christmas, after all, be what it had always been? Alena wondered when she saw the packages. She remembered the way Mother, bustling and merry, had always filled the house with wonderful smells at Christmastime. Well, this year, Alena had done that and could do more, she thought. She could mix up an applesauce cake tomorrow to bake while she cleaned the house. She could bring in sumac berries for the parlor table. On Christmas Eve, if Mother would not, she could pump out carols on the parlor organ and help the children hang their stockings and . . .

Alena was churning as she thought about Christmas. Now, of a sudden, she realized the butter had turned.

She lifted the crockery churn lid and began to gather the lumps of butter with the wooden paddle, all the while planning. The cake could be flavored with cinnamon, she thought, with hickory nuts scattered all through and the applesauce Aunt Louisa had brought them and . . .

"Sister," Faith was saying, tugging at her arm.

Alena looked up, feeling suddenly the cold Faith had brought with her into the kitchen. William and Fritz were still outside, stomping the snow from their boots against the back porch steps. Faith had not bothered, she saw. She had tracked snow, quickly turning into dirty puddles, across the floor that Alena had swept that morning.

"Faith!" she cried in exasperation. "Look what you've done! Were you born in a barn that you can't remember to wipe your boots?"

Faith looked at the muddy tracks. Her shoulders, in the worn coat handed down from Alena, slumped as she turned away. The sparkle in her eyes had faded.

"Sorry," she muttered. "I'll clean it up."

"What's to eat, Sister?" William and Fritz were shouting as they came through the door, letting in another draft of icy air.

Alena thought a moment, watching as Faith trudged back to take off her coat and mittens and scarves and hang them, alongside the boys', by the door.

"One gingerbread man apiece," she said, "and there's buttermilk, too, if you want."

Buttermilk was Faith's especial favorite, and the cookies were a treat, but Alena saw that Faith did not perk up. She dragged to the sink to fetch a rag and began to wipe up the wet footprints.

The boys brought the cookies from the pantry, jostling and gibing one another, and Alena poured them buttermilk from the crock. They gulped down the food and tore upstairs to change their clothes for chores.

Faith was rinsing her rag in the pan of water in the sink.

Alena wiped the last pale globs of butter from the paddle into a crockery bowl to be salted and worked smooth.

"I'm sorry, Faith," she said to Faith's back. "I didn't mean to be so sharp."

Faith turned, and Alena saw that she was crying.

"Oh, Faithie," Alena said, holding out her arms.

Faith ran to her, nearly bowling her over, and hugged her tight.

"I want my mother," Faith cried. "I want my mother when I come home from school."

"But Faithie," Alena said, dropping into a chair and pulling Faith, big as she was, onto her lap. "Mother is lying down right now."

"Wouldn't make no nevermind iffen she was up,"

cried Faith between big, gulping sobs. "I want her the way she used to be!"

Alena smoothed Faith's hair. She could feel the tears in her own eyes now.

"I know," she said, rocking Faith in her arms. "I know, I know."

There was nothing else to say.

Perhaps, Alena thought later, she expected a miracle. Miracles were supposed to happen at Christmas, weren't they?

There was a tree.

Father put it up while they slept, and it was there in the parlor, shining briefly with candles, when they came downstairs that morning. But Mother had not trimmed it. Alena could tell from the scantiness of the trimmings and the graceless way they were hung. Father had tried to make the tree beautiful, Alena could see, so she exclaimed with the other children when they saw it and said how wonderful it was. But it did not have Mother's touch.

There were presents.

The packages Father had brought from the village held pocketknives for William and Fritz, bright rubber balls for Delbert and Samuel, a pink parasol for Faith. For Alena there was a beautiful hat, a curve-brimmed sailor with blue velvet streamers. It was a hat for a young lady.

Father untied Mother's package for her and put into her hands a paisley silk shawl of red and blue and green. Mother let its soft folds run through her fingers and drop into her lap, unnoticed.

But there was no present for Father. Alena was ashamed that she had not remembered to knit him a scarf or hem-stitch a handkerchief or at least make him some pipe cleaners.

After church, there was dinner at Grandfather's house, as lavish as Thanksgiving.

But there were no miracles.

Mother was silent and vacant. Faith got sick on too much rich food. The little boys were cranky, the big ones rambunctious. Christmas had come and gone, and nothing had changed.

Sometimes of an evening, Alena helped the children with their schoolwork. William was quick with numbers and facts. Fritz plodded through his books as if he were ploughing stony ground. Faith could not spell to save her life. Alena enjoyed helping them, and she found she no longer resented staying at home. It is my duty, she told herself firmly. School was just a silly dream.

Still, she could not keep herself from reading. She read Father's *Tribune* and *The Youth's Companion* and the books in the glass-fronted case in the parlor. She read every night until her eyes would not stay open.

And then, in the daytime, while her hands were rubbing clothes on the washboard, she was sailing the ocean in *Two Years Before the Mast.* While her hands were sprinkling laundry, she was building tree houses with the Swiss Family Robinson. While her hands were kneading dough, she was playing on the shore with David Copperfield.

Inside Alena's head was adventure, mystery, romance.

Outside, nothing changed.

❧ 14 ❧

All Us Women

ON A RAW, windy Saturday in early spring, Alena woke with an ache in her belly. She could feel it, tight and heavy, across her abdomen and back and in her thighs. But she did not feel feverish, and her throat was not sore.

I can't be sick, she thought. If I were sick, someone else would have to do the cooking for the Sabbath. Who would Father send for? Mrs. Walt? Aunt Louisa or Aunt Sarah? One of the other aunts?

Alena lay in the warm nest of her covers, idly turning the thought in her mind. It would be nice to be sick. To stay abed all day and have someone bring her meals on a tray. To not have to go out in the wind to go to the privy, but be able to use the chamber pot and have someone else empty it. She would read, Alena thought. She would read all day, propped against her pillows, and someone would come and sit on the edge of the bed and ask how she felt and feel her forehead with a cool hand

and bring her something soothing to drink. Someone
. . . but who?

Alena sighed and threw back the covers, shivering in
the assault of the chill morning air.

It was Mother she wanted to do those things, she
realized. No, she couldn't be sick, for Mother wasn't
able.

She swung her legs over the side of the bed, steeling
herself for the cold of the floor. It was time to get up.

"Don't flag the covers, Sister!" Faith complained.
She was burrowing deeper into the warmth. Alena could
see only the top of her curly dark head.

Alena snatched up her clothes, and Faith's, to take
down to the kitchen to warm. She knew she was probably the first up this morning except for Father. She
woke now, out of habit, as soon as it began to get light.

In the kitchen, Alena dressed before the stove, turning first her front, then her back, to the fire Father had
built. She put on her underthings beneath the tent of
her nightdress, pulling it off only when she was ready to
pull on her dress.

The ache in her belly was deepening. Perhaps she
needed to go to the privy, she thought, wishing she did
not have to leave the fire. She put on her coat and
wrapped her head in a woolen scarf.

The wind almost pulled the door out of her hand
when she opened it. Leaning hard, she forced it closed

again. Then she put down her head and staggered across the yard.

The wind searched through her clothes with its icy fingers for every opening, however small. It reached down her neck and up her sleeves and whipped her skirts until she could feel it even on her legs. Suddenly she was aware of a wetness in her drawers, iced by the wind. Had she wet herself? she wondered, feeling ashamed. How could she have done such a thing without knowing?

The ache was a pain now. It doubled her over as she hurried across the yard, stumbling in wagon ruts and hoofprints that had been stiffened by the cold.

The privy was in the plum thicket, an unpainted one-holer. Alena opened the door and stepped in, grateful for the instant cessation of the wind, and grateful, too, that in wintertime the stench was not bad. She fastened the door, turned, and lifted the lid. The wind battered the little building and rattled the plum branches against its roof as she gathered up her skirts and fumbled for the buttons that fastened her drawers. Pulling them down, she settled on the cold wooden seat, holding her petticoats and skirt and apron and coat bunched on her lap. She could feel the cold against her thighs and feel an echo of the wind coming up through the hole to touch her bottom.

It was then, glancing at the drawers around her ankles, that Alena saw the stains. The gray flannel was smeared with blood. She stared at it in horror.

She was bleeding! Bleeding from *there*. Bleeding as Mother had done when she had the baby. Alena caught her breath. She could not pull her eyes away from the blood. Her head pounded with the thumping of the wind on the walls of the privy.

At last she began to breathe again. Her heart slowed, and an empty weakness in her knees and stomach replaced the first terror. Little by little, she began to think, to hold her thoughts carefully still as she stilled her trembling legs.

Surely she could not be having a baby! She was too young—though she did remember that Cordelia Bagley had gotten married to old Mr. Rees Andrews when she was only fourteen, and she had had a baby the very next year. But Alena was not married. A girl couldn't have a baby unless she was married . . . or could she? Alena racked her brain, trying to remember what folks had said about Olive May Davies when she went away so sudden to visit her aunt in Omaha.

It can't be a baby, Alena thought. I must be hurt. *Be hurt, be hurt,* beat her heart. I must be hurt, but how? She swallowed hard and forced her eyes away from the stains on her drawers.

Then came the shame. This was even worse than wetting herself. Something dreadful must have hap-

pened to her. And if it wasn't a baby, what could it be?
There was the blood. There was the pain in her belly.
Just like Mother. . . .

She should look, Alena thought. She should look to
see what was wrong with her. But she could not. She
had never looked at herself . . . *there.* Or touched herself.
She did not know *how* she knew, but she knew that to
look, to touch herself, was not a nice thing to do. Was
an immodest, perhaps even sinful thing to do.

Alena tore a page from the mail-order catalog, which
hung by a string from a nail on the wall. She crumpled
it in her fingers until it was soft and wiped carefully
between her legs. The paper was bloody, but the pain
was deep inside her. It was her insides that were bleeding. She dropped the paper down the hole and felt sick
with shame.

Alena forced herself to think. What must I do? she
thought. What had Mother done that night?

She asked *me* for help!

Suddenly the longing for Mother, for Mother as she
used to be, was so sharp it reduced the pain in her
belly to nothing. Alena remembered the comfort of
Mother's hands, the safeness of her arms. She remembered the way Mother had looked at her the night
Matilda Jane was born, as though she and Alena had
shared the birthing. As though, together, they had done
something wonderful, something only they two could

have done. She had felt so close to Mother then. . . .

But *that* Mother was gone, she thought, the thought leaden. Gone, gone, gone . . .

Hunched on the privy seat, Alena began to rock, backward and forward, silently.

Alena dragged back across the yard, the wind pushing against her back. She felt like an old woman, feeble and bent. In the shelter of the porch, she stopped and looked through the window into the kitchen before she pushed open the door. No one was there. Father must be in the barn, milking perhaps, and the children not yet up. Faith's clothes were still on the chair by the stove where she had left them to warm.

Alena closed the door behind her softly. She did not want them to hear her, not yet. Avoiding the treads that creaked, she crept upstairs.

In their room, Faith still slept. Alena tiptoed to the chest. In the bottom drawer was an old petticoat, she remembered. She had outgrown it long since, but it was still too big for Faith. The dreadful waste of it gave her pause as she dug beneath the neatly folded summer cottons, searching for it. She closed her eyes a moment, gritted her teeth, and drew it out.

It can't be helped, she thought, and began to tear it into squares. The ripping sounded loud to her ears, and she stole a glance at Faith, who did not stir. Her heart thumped as she tore the petticoat across and across again and folded a square into a pad as she had seen Mrs. Walt do after Mother had the baby. Then, stripping off her bloody drawers, she bound the pad between her legs with strips torn from the petticoat—again as Mrs. Walt had done for Mother—and pulled on a clean pair of drawers. When she had buttoned them with trembling fingers, she sank down in the chair and hugged herself to stop her shaking. She felt cold, so cold, but she realized she had not taken off her coat.

Faith would think it strange if she woke and saw her sitting there in her coat, the bloody drawers and sacrificed petticoat in ruins at her feet. Swiftly she gathered the remnants of the petticoat and stuffed them back into the drawer beneath their summer underthings. Then she wadded the drawers into a ball and, pulling off her coat, hid them in its folds and tiptoed from the room. She had some idea of washing them, later, when no one could see.

On the landing, her coat hugged in her arms, Alena stopped to take stock. Her skin was goose-bumpy with chill, and her hands still shook, but with the pad to staunch and hide the bleeding, she felt better. The pain . . . why, the pain had gone, Alena realized suddenly. She remembered that there had been long moments the night the baby was born when Mother's pain had seemed to abate, too. She stood still and waited for it to seize her again. She waited and waited. . . .

When Mother's door swung open, Alena started guiltily and clutched her coat to her breast. Mother stood in the doorway in her nightdress, her hair disheveled. She was blinking slowly, looking at Alena with a question in her eyes.

Alena knew what the question was. In a moment, Mother would say it in that hollow, heartbreaking voice. "Alena," Mother would say, "where is the baby?"

Suddenly, Alena could not bear it, could not bear to tell her once more that the baby was gone. Gone to heaven, the children always said when Mother asked them. Gone, Mary, gone, can't you understand? Father would say in despair. But standing there on the landing, waiting for the question, Alena could not bear to answer it one more time and then gently steer Mother back to bed or help her to get dressed. Not now! Not ever again!

"She's *dead*, Mother," Alena said before Mother even asked. "Dead, dead, *dead*!" Alena was shouting now. "And I'm sorry, Mother, and so is everyone else, but it can't be helped! The baby doesn't need you anymore, Mother. *We* need you. *I* need you! Now! I need you right *now*!"

Alena was crying so hard she could not choke out another word. She was crying and shaking, and Mother stood before her, maddeningly blank and swaying a little in the onslaught of her anger. Alena slapped her . . . hard.

In the silence that followed that awful resounding

slap, Alena thought she heard the sound of her own heart breaking. All, all was in ruins now, and *she* had done it. The bleeding, the anger, the violence of that slap—*her* hand hitting *Mother!*—had destroyed her careful patching of the torn fabric of their lives. She had been trying to mend things, she thought, but she hadn't the strength or skill. She never would have a woman's skill!

Alena's knees gave way, and she sat suddenly on the floor of the landing and buried her face in the coat clutched in her arms and cried. There was nothing in the world but Alena's crying. Nothing but the racking sobs that ripped at her throat, nothing but the scalding tears.

Then there *was* something. There was something strong and warm—arms about her, a murmuring voice. Mother was kneeling beside her, holding her and rocking her and crying with her.

Mother.

"Having a baby, Alena? Why, don't be silly," Mother said. "You're not having a baby. It's your monthly is all. I've been meaning to tell you . . ." Mother's voice, which was sounding so sensible and calm, so like Mother as she used to be, trailed off. She put her hand to her forehead and closed her eyes a moment. Then, "I meant to tell you before now," she said, "but I seem to have been . . ."

Alena hugged her. "It's all right, Mother," she said.

"You've been grieving for the baby, grieving for Matilda Jane. We all have."

Tears were trickling from beneath Mother's closed eyelids. She and Alena had been crying and crying. This was the first crying Mother and she had done for the baby. Perhaps Mother had not been grieving. Perhaps that was part of the trouble. It was as though she had been asleep all this time.

Mother's eyes were open again, open and filled with concern. "Alena, it's something that happens to all us women, this bleeding every month. It's a wonderful thing really. It means that you are growing up, that God is preparing you to have babies someday. But not now. Not now, dear. Not until you are ready."

Alena nodded, but she could not stop the tears that continued to course down her cheeks. It was as though all the fear, all the burden she had been carrying, was flowing out of her. Moment by moment, she was lightening, but she wanted to hear it again.

"But the pain," she said. "I have a pain here." She put her hand on her belly and realized that the pain had not come back. "I *had* a pain," she said.

Mother smiled through her tears. Smiled! Alena had forgotten how radiant Mother's smile could be.

"Sometimes there is a little cramping pain, right at first," Mother said, "to get your monthly started. But I've never had a speck of trouble with mine, and I don't reckon you will either. Don't be afraid."

"I'm not," Alena said, shaking her head. "I'm not afraid." It was the truth. For the first time in a long time, Alena was not afraid.

"Mary! 'Lena!" Father was bounding up the steps toward them, three at a time. "What's amiss?" he was crying.

Alena realized how she and Mother must look, all in a heap on the floor of the landing, their faces wet and their eyes red and their noses running, smiling at each other. She began to giggle.

Mother looked at her, and then Mother began to laugh.

"Nothing," Alena gasped to her astonished father.

"Nothing, Clay," Mother said, putting out her arms to Father.

"Nothing at all's amiss!"

✻ *15* ✻

Butterflies

ALENA COULD SEE Mrs. Malcolm on the porch. There was no one else in sight. Nervously, Alena patted her pocket. The recipe was still there, the recipe for plum pudding that Mrs. Malcolm had asked Mother for this morning at church. The crispness of the paper it was written on heartened Alena. She did have a reason for coming, she thought. She was doing Mother's bidding. Besides, most likely Mr. Malcolm was not at home. His mother sat alone, in a straight-backed chair, in the shade of her porch, reading something, Alena saw. She had changed from her Sunday-best purple to a plain gray dress. It made her seem less imposing.

Alena straightened her shoulders and started up their lane. She would just give Mrs. Malcolm the recipe and leave, she thought. "You'd best stay awhile and visit," Mother had said, "to be polite." But Alena knew the recipe was an excuse. What Mother was hoping was that Alena would talk to Mr. Malcolm about school.

The children had already started school this fall, and Mother had urged Alena to go with them. But Alena was reluctant. She felt too old now, with the girls her own age graduated. Violet said she was overjoyed to be finished and free. Minnie was living with a married sister, helping take care of her nephews and niece. Adaline had started high school in the village. Besides, Mother needed Alena.

It was true that Mother was recovering from her long illness—that was how Alena thought of it now, an illness. But though Mother grew stronger every day, it was also true that there would be another baby late in the fall. And this time, Alena meant to see that Mother did not overdo.

At first, after that day last spring when she had come to herself, Mother had been weak, easily tired and overwrought. For a long time, things went on much as they had—Alena minding the house and the children, with Mother only helping as she was able. But as spring passed into summer, more and more it was Mother who took charge, and Alena who helped. This time, as Mother grew bigger with the baby, she grew rosier and livelier, too, it seemed to Alena. Alena meant that she should keep on that way. She could not imagine leaving Mother again to do all the work herself.

No, Alena could not picture herself going off to school now, not grade school, and anyway there seemed no point. She couldn't leave Mother to go to normal school either, even if she could get a scholarship.

But Mother kept after her. "I'm so much better now," she said. "It wouldn't hurt to just ask."

There would be no opportunity to ask, Alena thought now with relief as she set her foot on the bottom step of the Malcolms' front porch. Mr. Malcolm was not at home. She would give the recipe to his mother and go.

"Good day, Alena," Mrs. Malcolm was saying, looking up from her book—a Bible, Alena saw, a big, leather-bound Bible.

"Hello, Mrs. Malcolm," Alena said. "My mother sent over the recipe you wanted."

"How thoughtful of her to be so prompt. Next Sunday at church would have sufficed."

Alena could see where Mr. Malcolm got his formal way of speaking. She remembered that some of the church ladies said that Mrs. Malcolm put on airs.

Mrs. Malcolm was indicating another chair, a white wicker one, with her tiny, plump hand. "Will you sit awhile?"

"I only just came to bring the recipe," Alena said. "My mother needs me to come straight home."

"Well, then . . ."

Mrs. Malcolm held out her hand, and Alena fumbled in her pocket for the slip of paper.

The screen door creaked, and Alena jumped and dropped the recipe. As she bent to retrieve it, the breeze caught it and sent it fluttering across the porch. Alena lunged after it and found herself on her hands and knees, looking at a pair of immaculate black boots. The recipe, crumpled now, was clutched in her fingers.

"Good afternoon, Miss Ostermann," came Mr. Malcolm's voice from above her.

She felt his hand under her elbow, helping her up, but she could not bring herself to look into his face.

"I thought I heard your voice," Mr. Malcolm said.

"Mrs. Ostermann sent Alena over with a recipe for me," said Mrs. Malcolm.

Alena nodded dumbly, her face scarlet.

"I'm glad to see you," said Mr. Malcolm. "I've been looking for an opportunity to speak to you."

"Alena can't stay," said Mrs. Malcolm, her voice abrupt.

"Then may I walk you a ways, Miss Ostermann?" Mr. Malcolm said, taking the crumpled paper from Alena and handing it to his frowning mother with a slight bow.

Still Alena could not speak.

"I'll be back soon, Mother," Mr. Malcolm said.

Alena found herself walking back down the lane with Mr. Malcolm at her side. Her heart was fluttering unevenly, and it was difficult to breathe. She had not been this close to Mr. Malcolm, or spoken to him, since that day last year when she told him she was quitting school. As they walked, Alena could see that he was shortening his stride to match hers.

"Is your mother well, Miss Ostermann?" he said as they turned out of the lane.

Alena nodded. "Yes," she said, "much better, thank you." Her voice sounded breathless and shaky, she thought. She tried again. "Much better."

"We have missed you at school."

Silence.

Alena could not think what to answer. Finally, "Me, too," she said, swallowing hard.

"Will you be returning soon?"

Alena looked down at the road. Dust puffed from beneath her shoes. She could feel the perspiration spreading in wet circles under her arms.

"No," she said. "I'm afraid not. My mother needs me. They all . . . All the family needs me. There are so many of us and Mother's expecting . . ."

Alena felt herself flush hot and red. She had not meant to blurt *that* out.

"I . . . I mean . . ."

"I see," said Mr. Malcolm, and she could hear the disapproval icy in his voice.

"*We're* all delighted!" Alena said sharply, suddenly angry. Who was he to disapprove of Mother, of her family? "We're happy about it. Very!"

He inclined his head. "I see."

"No, you don't see," said Alena. "There are more important things than school, you know. Books aren't real life. *Life!* That's what's important. I'm *needed!*"

Silence again, and Alena wanted to sink into the ground. What had possessed her? What was she saying? The truth was, she had wanted to go to school more than anything in the world, only it was too late. There was no sense fooling herself.

Alena stopped and held her hand out to Mr. Malcolm.

"I can go on from here alone," she said. "Thank you for walking with me and . . . and thank you for . . . for asking about . . ."

Mr. Malcolm did not take her hand. Instead he looked at her intently.

"Miss Ostermann," he said, "it would be a great waste if you do not continue your studies. I . . . I *personally* would think it a shame . . . But I *do* understand that your family needs you. One owes one's mother . . . It is not easy, I know. When your parents want one thing for you, and you want something else . . . Compromises must be made. I, too . . . Miss Ostermann, I think you most unselfish. Most . . . noble, truly, to sacrifice . . . It's just that . . ."

Mr. Malcolm seemed distraught. Alena was astonished. She looked at him, her mouth open a little, trying to take in his meaning.

"Miss Ostermann, if I prepared some lessons for you, some reading to do at home, would you . . . would you consider . . . I'd be so happy if I could help you. Then, perhaps, someday . . . One never knows. Circumstances do change. There's always the chance that . . . that you might be able to go on, to take the teaching examination perhaps, or . . ."

Alena could feel her tears welling. She was caught, like a fish on a hook, by the concern in his eyes. They gazed into hers, unblinking, earnest, blotting out the rest of the world. She could not think, could not . . . A tear quivered, fell, and Alena dashed it away with the back of her hand.

"I didn't mean it," she said. "Books *are* important. For me, they are part of life."

"I know," said Mr. Malcolm. "For me also. . . ."

"I have to go," said Alena. "I really do have to go."

"Yes," said Mr. Malcolm, looking down and releasing her from his gaze. "Alena," he said, his voice low, "please, may I help?"

He had called her by her name. Alena, he had said.

"I'd be obliged," said Alena, her heart suddenly singing, in spite of herself.

Mr. Malcolm nodded briskly and held out his hand.

"That's settled then," he said. "Don't despair, Miss Ostermann. We'll find a way."

Alena smiled, her lips trembling. She could not trust herself to speak. She put out her hand and felt his fingers close over hers, briefly, warmly.

Then he turned and strode away.

* * *

Alena shuffled her feet through the yellow aspen leaves that littered the side of the road. The world was flaunting its finery one last time, she thought, before it was disrobed by winter. The oaks, black and red, wore gowns of garnet, the hawthorns gowns of ruby, the cottonwoods gold. At their feet were carpets of purple asters and tawny grass, heavy with seed. Overhead, Alena heard wild geese calling. She looked into the light of the lowering sun and saw the black vees of their wings beating southward. The air smelled like cider, she thought.

It was getting late. The angle of the sun reminded her that she needed to get home. She would take a shortcut through the orchard, she decided. It was quicker than the road. She hiked up her skirts, clambered over the fence, and set off across the stubble of the timothy field.

She was trying not to think of her talk with Mr. Malcolm. If she thought too hard about it, she might discover it hadn't happened the way she remembered. She wanted to keep it safe, unexamined, in some hidden place within her. She feared it could not stand the light, and yet, she could not think of anything else. Everything paled beside the memory of those moments—the gaudy trees, the sun slipping behind the horizon, everything.

A way might yet be found, Mr. Malcolm had said, to follow her dream, the dream that Matilda Jane's birth had interrupted. No, it had not been Matilda Jane. It had been life. Life had gotten between Alena and her dream as, she suddenly realized, life must have interfered somehow with Mr. Malcolm's hopes. It was best not to hope, Alena told herself. Then one could not be disappointed. She would think of something else—of the petticoat she was embroidering for Faith. She would use purple for the flowers, like the asters, she thought.

As Alena neared the Osage hedge that surrounded the apple orchard, she heard a sound. She had been hearing it for some time, she realized, but it had been so faint she had not been aware. Now it was growing louder, a whisper, a murmur somewhere above her. She shielded her eyes against the glare of the setting sun and saw a cloud descending from the heavens. It was the cloud that was whispering, louder and louder. The cloud was obscuring the light. Alena squinted, frowning. What . . . ?

Wings were swirling around her, orange and sable, flashing with sunlight. Alena put up her hands and felt them brush against her, softly, tingling against her skin.

Butterflies! They were all about her, a great cloud of monarch butterflies, settling onto the hedge. She stood in their breathing center, and her heart beat with their wings.

This was what she had meant, she knew suddenly, when she had told Mr. Malcolm that *life* was the important thing. Life was like these butterflies, fragile and brief, and death was in it, as it was in them. Alena

remembered the butterfly Delbert had found. She remembered the disappointing emptiness of the hedge
that Faith had seen cloaked with living butterflies. She
remembered Matilda Jane.

Yet, the butterflies were back. Not the same ones,
perhaps, but others, as another baby would be born. For
each butterfly who died on its journey, another would
crawl from its chrysalis to stretch its damp wings in the
sunlight. Its journey might not be easy. The winds
might tatter its wings. The rains might drench it. The
heat might be merciless as it flew. But fly it would,
however briefly, and take joy in the flight, in the sunlight and nectar and in its own beauty.

The butterflies had settled on the hedge, making it
blossom with orange and black, like living, moving
flowers. Alena's throat was tight and aching with their
loveliness, and with their sadness, and with the bravery
of their flight.

She *could* hope, she thought. That was what Mr.
Malcolm had been trying to say to her. She could live
each day as best she could, loving and helping those who
needed her, and still have something for herself. It
would not take anything from the family if she read and
studied when she had the time. It would not harm anyone if she dreamed.

For that was what life was also, Alena finally saw. Not
just birth and death, joy and pain, love and duty, but

also hope. If it was too late to go back to school, it was not too late to find another dream. It was never too late to hope.

The sun was down. In the violet dusk, the wings of the butterflies whispered courage to Alena. She slipped through the opening in the hedge and went toward the lights of home.

A Note to the Reader

WHEN I WAS a little girl, my grandmother and great-aunt Ruth (in this story she is called Faith) used to tell me about their family. They said there were nine children. Yet when I counted the great-aunts and great-uncles and my grandmother, there were only eight. This was a mystery until I found a list of the brothers and sisters. In addition to the ones I knew, there was Matilda, born November 21, 1886, died November 23, 1886. Three days! I was astonished. This baby sister had lived only three days, and yet they always counted her one of the family.

Granny also used to tell me about the abysmal ignorance in which girls of her generation were kept regarding the "facts of life": menstruation, sexuality, birth.

When she was ninety years old, Auntie Ruth wrote a "memory book," in which she told many details about farm life near Elvaston (Hancock County), Illinois, in the 1880s and 1890s. She told of "finding in the fall on the north side of the tall Osage hedge around the orchard . . . a beautiful robe of monarch butterflies, resting . . . on their way to California to spend the winter."

She also told of all the work involved in farm life for her mother and "sister Alena":

Our dear mother . . . went calmly about her numerous daily tasks—as a wife, over 9 rooms—3 daily farm meals to get, mother of 9 children, hired men to cook for, all the sewing to do for the family (we did not buy ready-made clothing those days), canning of all our fruit, washing and ironing each week. . . . And our Saturdays were devoted to preparing meals for the Sabbath day. . . . Mother and Alena cooked great roasts, plates of some kind of fowl, baked 8 or 10 big fragrant loaves of bread, 7 or 8 pies, a big fancy cake, puddings and what have you, so Sunday would not be just another workday. . . .

From these fragments, this story has been fashioned, in memory of that hardworking and loving mother, Mary Martin Rohrbough, and her daughters: big sister Alena; little Ruth (Faith); the baby who died, Matilda; and a baby yet unborn, Edith, my grandmother.

Ellen Howard
Beaverton, Oregon
September 20, 1989